CHOOSE
EDUCATION
OVER CRIME

TOOLS AND STRATEGIES
TO SAVE OUR YOUTH

Ronald Alexander M.Ed.

PAGE PUBLISHING, INC.
Conneaut Lake, PA

First originally published by Page Publishing 2021

ISBN 978-1-6624-2580-6 (pbk)
ISBN 978-1-6624-2581-3 (digital)

Printed in the United States of America

My name is Ronald L. Alexander Sr. I am writing this book because I feel compelled to share the plethora of knowledge I obtained in twenty-five-plus years of service in education. During this time, under my leadership, I improved four schools per state testing.

I began my educational journey as a lunch aide and followed the educational flowchart—teacher, academic coach, and principal, until reaching the position of director of education. As a director, I accomplished the following tasks: I developed two computer labs through donations, with over eighty computers for one site; envisioned a space on the school's property for better student use and created a soccer field; turned a school with a D rating into a B-rated school; assisted in creating one of the most extensive school-wide title programs in the state, under the guidance and leadership of Maverik Education and founder, Erik Francis; increased testing participation throughout the district by 50 percent; created an effective management plan used to eliminate 80 percent of school referrals, detentions, school suspensions. And yet the achievement gap continues to grow.

Although I hope the strategies I provide can be useful to *all* educators, I am explicitly targeting inner-city schools, parents, teachers, districts, and minority students.

For most of my career, I have worked with economically disadvantaged students, mostly minority students in the inner city, because they continue to be afflicted by the inequalities within education.

As an administrator, you are continually reviewing and analyzing data to make decisions that should have a positive impact on your campus. However, when I became a high school principal, I was overwhelmed at the schools' data. Nothing caught my attention more than the number of underperforming students and the attrition rate for all demographics within the state of Arizona. Ten-thousand-plus students a year drop out of school in Arizona, and the trajectory seems to continue upward. When this occurs, the state and schools lose millions, if not billions, over a lifetime, which has a drastic effect on resources that could have been purchased to improve education in Arizona.

Historically, we believed it took a village to raise a child, but that belief has devolved, especially within the Black race, as it pertains to education. Now when schools are underperforming, it just appears to be a cycle of blame because no one wants to accept ownership for failure. I do not understand why this is the case because there is nothing wrong with not achieving success immediately. Some of our most outstanding leaders discuss how failure has led them to becoming successful. The real issue with loss is allowing yourself to accept it. When teachers have difficulty communicating with students and parents, parents struggle to communicate with children and the community blames them both because of the violence and disrespect they endure from all. You can say a toxic culture and environment is established within your community/school.

Unfortunately, many schools within the inner city continue to struggle with exiting the black hole of underperformance. Due to an array of leadership, direction, and belief changes, staff members and students gradually moves into a stage of confinement, assuming this is as good as it gets.

As educators, we must display a positive attitude regarding education. Students should be academically ready to enter the workforce and compete for job opportunities without the contriteness of assuming they are not prepared to be productive employees.

Within the last three years, I have witnessed hundreds of students and multiple staff members confined to their current existence without doing better. It appears as though teachers have found comfort in failing as long as their pay continues while students are losing value and interest in school. When this occurs, it plays a significant role in why failure continues.

Now, there are many other reasons why a school fails, and it is not always due to the student. I am just more concerned with the items that I can control. As I mentioned before, many leaders avoid accepting blame, but *true* leaders take the glory and shame because they know how to convert the latter into credit. That is called instructional leadership. If you are at the top, say a superintendent or a chief executive officer, and you are not an instructional leader, then you should at least know how to lead members of your team.

To change a failing school's status, one must accept the cold-hearted truth about why students are failing. At times throughout this book, I may say something that is not so pleasing to the ear, but it is not with the intent that I try to upset you. It is just the truth, and together we can turn negative student achievement around.

In the last eight years of my career, I have been astounded with the number of students who continue to value street life over a good education. We must save our youth! I have spoken to so many students who have no fear of prison life, probation, or even death. I do not think this is what they want for themselves, but unfortunately, based on the daily experiences they encounter, they feel trapped with no way out. In their eyes, school is their last option before heading toward a life of crime. Even if they do not value school currently, if they are still coming that is a sign that they want help. We can't afford to let felonies replace diplomas and degrees for our youth. Their institution of learning must come from a school, not prison.

Below, I have taken the time to address a few topics that I hope will serve as a guide and benefit to all inner-city school districts, leaders, parents, teachers, and community members. Whenever I am called as a principal or consultant in need of assisting a school, the first item I investigate is culture.

Culture

Several leaders still may not understand the importance of a positive culture and how it should be used to drive everything else. I have been blessed as a leader in knowing its importance, so it is the first item I render if needed. In 2018, I was told by my AdvancED auditors, an accreditation organization, that they could not believe what I have achieved with turning the behavior of the school around given the negativity stated in the last report. While impressed with my accomplishments, the school and its infrastructure still did not do so well with their findings. I was within my fourth month of being a principal at that time.

When there is a positive culture, *all* stakeholders are on the same page and you will be able to identify that learning is the focus. When parents know their children will be safe and learning will occur, they will drive their children across the city to attend your school.

A positive culture can eliminate minor concerns impeding progress for school improvement. You will never be able to reach your vision or mission when your culture is not positive. When you fail, success requires more work and some staff members may not be interested in change (confinement).

I remember when I took over an alternative school as principal, in December I might add, and it just so happened another leader for the school was sharing the building with me and arrived at the same time as I did. We remembered each other from the Department of Education, but it has been a while since we worked in the same field, school improvement. When he asked me what my plan was, I told him I would address culture first, which would reduce or eliminate cursing, and then address training teachers to improve academics within the school.

At no time did I address or care about previous information as to why the school was in this predicament. I took the next six months to focus on the items I mentioned to my colleague. Over time, he witnessed the culture gradually changing but still was not convinced. I knew because I would check in with him to see if he was noticing a difference.

Next, cursing diminished at least up to 90 percent before the year ended. I told staff members that when they get back, we were going to change our teaching style, but first, we must review our roles. I know for a fact that when an organizational chart in an under-performing school is not established and expected to be followed, the plan will not work. Once we had been over the chart and everyone's role, I went into training mode.

As a leader, it is crucial that you know what to attack and limit the items you want to change. You may have ten concerns, but not *all* can be rectified at once. Many leaders fall when not following this rule because they are doing too much. I truly hope this info helps. I respect and appreciate all my peers. As a leader, I practice what I preach, so if I tell teachers to chunk content for a better understanding, then that rule applies to me.

The following year, our school passed the state assessment per AzMERIT score in 2018. Students were awarded eight scholarships with Paradise Valley Community College, all seniors were offered jobs through one of the partnerships that I developed, and all seniors for that year graduated.

Once I demonstrated success, I had staff members and students believe in the drive and support it. One parent was so impressed with the change I made in his child and others that he went on a mission to elicit funds for our school. He donated 10K for the cause, and in turn, I gave it to the school's charter holder. It was the first time that has ever been done for the school, and they have been open for twenty years. My colleagues and I still laugh to this day about what we accomplished. I definitely could not have achieved this success without him or the teachers, so I would like to shout them out for such an accomplishment. Paul, Sharanita, William, Jeffery, Ryan, Claribel, Crystal, and Devaughn, thank you.

Unfortunately, we received a new leader the following year, and she relocated me to the school where her husband was the principal because it was experiencing discipline issues. I was reluctant to move based on my previous success and all the partnerships I just developed, but I was informed I had no choice. Just like the beginning of the previous school mentioned, Dr. Paul was also relocated and placed in this school before my arrival. When Claribel, the school registrar, and I relocated, we put the same plan into effect. I was a little more worried about this school based on some of the things I had heard, but I had a plan. As a leader, I know you either have a plan or you plan to fail. Failure was not an option for our youth under my watch. Like before, the staff and I turned the behavior and culture around to create a positive environment for student learning. Again, staff members were astounded at the results. Students went from taking drugs to reading aloud, completing assignments, respecting one another and staff members while enjoying learning. The students raved about the changes. Under my guidance, I could get students back on track and in line with graduation requirements. Students were extremely grateful and showed their appreciation by doing their work. The atmosphere was positive because staff members saw hope and knew they were working in an environment where everyone cared about the students' welfare.

My point is that a positive culture will make students work for themselves and those who helped in making a positive change in their life. People would often ask, How did you change that school around when they know what the school was like beforehand? I would always respond with the great words of Madeline Hunter, "Students do not care how much you know until they know how much you care." Thank you, guru Madeline Hunter!

Relationships

If you are not an educator, I am unsure if you know how new buzz terms seem to be the key to all concerns regarding education. The school year 2019–2020 buzz term is relationships. So many people believe that if teachers have a relationship with their students then all other concerns will disappear.

Do not get me wrong. Relationships are essential, but you do not have time to form relationships when you are underperforming. That should not even be the focus and here is why. Relationships are based on emotions, and just as much as there are positive relationships, there are also negative relationships. Isn't this why we have divorce, murder, abuse, bullying, and hatred?

We have to understand that, as a school, you cannot continue to circle around the exact reason you were given permission to exist, which is to educate children. There is nothing on standardized assessments about relationships. Please adhere to focusing on the learning. When teachers focus on the learning, behavior improves, classroom disruptions decrease, and student performance increases. It truly is a simple formula that works every time.

Usually, when you see teachers who do not seem to have a rapport/relationship with their students, it is because they do not know how to acquire a rapport/relationship with an inner-city student. One thing about inner-city students is that they smell bullshit right away. When you are either a product of your environment or attempting not to become a product of your environment, you learn how to scan people to avoid any harm you could encounter.

Forming a relationship with a student who lives in poverty, who, at times, starve for food, who regularly fight the negativity of their world and a host of other setbacks will not be easy. However, if teachers train on addressing students with specific characteristics, you can be successful.

Unfortunately, this is easier said than done. Most teachers feel they already know how to interact with ALL students. When I received a new staff member and asked if he ever worked at an Alternative School, he replied "I worked with these types of kids for years." Well, there lies the first problem. What do you mean "these types of students"?

Here is an example of what occurs when you do not know how to form a rapport with an inner-city student. You must be aware that when working with junior high students or high school students, they do not like being embarrassed. The teacher entered my school and assumed he knew how to work with alternative inner-city students because of his experience somewhere else with students like these. (There is that phrase again.)

One day, a student was talking about drinking alcohol during class (first red flag). The teacher was listening to the conversation and decided to indulge (second red flag), assuming he had a relationship with the student and said, "What are you? An alcoholic? Or do you have alcoholics in your family?"

Needless to say, the student went ballistic, and the teacher attempted to write the student up for his behavior. I, in turn, wrote the teacher up, stating that his behavior was unprofessional and that he had no right to ask the student that question. He told me he was being sarcastic and did not mean anything by it. What he did not realize was that his sarcasm destroyed any opportunity to acquire a relationship with this student for the remainder of the year. Since that day, the teacher has had issues with that student.

Now, if learning was the focus of this classroom, this would have never occurred because students would have known the room, school, and teacher expectations.

Discipline

Till this day, teachers are spending more time on behavior than teaching. I began school in 1975, and it was during the era of corporal punishment (CP). I know many people out there are against corporal punishment, and 90 percent of them have never experienced it.

Let me tell you how inner-city students in my era viewed corporal punishment. It was another form of discipline. There were still suspensions, detentions, and even in school suspensions. Swatting was the result before being removed from school to prevent removal from occurring. CP was never viewed as abuse. Isn't abuse caused by someone who dislikes you or does not care about you in a positive light? If so, I do not understand how people refer to CP as abuse. Corporal punishment is for something you did. Abuse has nothing to do with anything you may have done; therefore, there is no comparison.

I am not saying that CP cures all discipline issues in school. I am saying that it establishes some fear in students when thinking about the consequences and makes them change his/her mind before doing wrong. For example, if swatted for cursing out the teacher, most students would choose another direction to take.

Now removed from the schools, teachers get cursed out daily because everything else in education evolved but discipline. Students are not worried about detentions, suspensions, or anything else regarding consequences. They hope you put them out of school to be free from obligations such as behaving, doing their work, respecting the teacher, and other items.

Again, if you focus on the learning and allow that to control the environment, I promise you will not be disappointed. Most students who attend school want to learn, but that is often taken away from them due to the constant distractions occurring during the learning process.

Classroom management does not determine if you are a good teacher or not. Some people do not like being assertive to or reprimanding someone else's child. If that is the case, the school or administrator of the school should have an effective management plan that would support the teacher. An EMP levels the playing field for all students. Students who get in the most trouble have already been labeled despite having a disability or not. An EMP holds students accountable for their actions without the need for yelling or screaming at the student. The critical aspect of a sufficient EMP is the follow through. If done correctly, you cannot fail. I have used this method in schools from the Midwest to the west coast, and it works to perfection. Please ask any of my teachers who have experienced this process under my leadership.

Parents, I hope this information reaches for the purpose in which it was intended: to assist in providing your child a solid education. I understand that you face many challenges in raising your family, but if we can work together in educating your child, I am sure it can provide you some relief. To assist with my delivery, I created an alphabetical word list that has always served me well as an administrator when communicating with parents. Some of the words listed may not pertain to you, but please take full advantage if useful.

Attendance

Parents, please, please, please understand that your child cannot pass school by being absent. Many parents call the school to report the child's absence, and although that is the right thing to do, it should not continuously cause the student to miss weeks throughout the term. If your child's school operates in quarters and he/she misses three to four weeks, they automatically fail because the quarter is only nine weeks. Therefore, they missed half the term and work needed for a passing grade.

As an administrator, I often hear parents ask about makeup when the child missed school. Makeup is right for a day or two but not weeks at a time. If students could pass class just by doing makeup work, why come?

The following categories should be used to determine a student's overall grade: attendance, participation, passing scores on graded work, homework, test, and quizzes. When students miss out on school, they also miss out on all items contributing to their grade.

Attitude

The more positive you are when communicating with the school or teacher, the more positive its effect will have on your child as a student. When you yell, threaten, or even curse an employee out in front of your child, it demonstrates to your child that we are not aligned and that he/she does not have to respect the teacher or staff members.

This indifference can harm your child while attending school. Often, they are so embarrassed they no longer participate in the learning. Ensure you force the teacher to grade the student's abilities and not the negative interaction that occurs between you and the teacher whenever the teacher calls you.

Bullying

Bullying has become a significant issue in schools. Students are forced into doing things outside of their character just to fit in. Today, bullying comes in many forms, and by the time you are aware it is occurring with your child, the damage has been done. As an administrator, I am concerned with some of the actions students take due to bullying because of how life-threatening they are, such as cutting themselves.

This is something I was never exposed to as a student; however, it appears to be shared today. It is imperative that we communicate with our children and be aware of any changes that could allude to them cutting themselves. As an administrator, the clues I used to determine if I should be concerned with the child's welfare are if the student always wears dark clothing as if to appear gothic; if the student always has their arms covered regardless of how hot it was; or if the student will always rub their arms as if the cut was still fresh and irritating their skin. Communication is the key to stopping bullying. Where many schools fail is when they only announce that they ban bullying or discuss consequences for bullying instead making it a part of the daily learning.

Counseling

If your child needs counseling and is not receiving it at school, but he/she is a special education student, then there is a problem. If provided, it would benefit you as the parent and your child to know what services have been agreed upon and monitor them. You can accomplish this by merely keeping record of services rendered. The log will help guide some of the meeting discussions on services being rendered and its effectiveness.

Counseling should be provided by a certified counselor who can offer you the medical/emotional strategies needed to assist with your child's concern. Unfortunately, many schools have been providing pseudo services by hiring companies who can only talk to your children about their problems. This strategy can cause more damage than good based on the lack of professional skills needed for the concern. I also do not understand how a noncertified organization can provide services for a student with medical issues and still mandate that those services remain confidential. Basically, when this occurs, your child is being provided someone they can vent to about their trouble. Although needed, the goal is to develop strategies that would limit the concern to benefit from their learning.

Credit Analysis

This is a very important section for any parent who needs assistance tracking their child's classes throughout their high school journey. The form also allows you to track your child's GPA to determine their school status. Typically, somebody would do this for you, the school counselor, but when your school does not provide a counselor, it is the students responsibility to track this data.

Students are not ready to choose the correct classes in sequence to prepare them for their career of choice, and when they are forced to do so, it usually results in them elongating their graduation date due to taking non-relevant courses for the job they are aiming for. Some schools have the registrar assist with this task, but they are not trained in knowing this information either. In most cases, they are just reading from a list of classes that relates to a particular career.

It may not seem important to you, but this is why guidance counselors are in place. Even if the student attends college, it is suggested that one allows the guidance counselor to prepare their schedule.

There are many students, especially in alternative charter high schools, who have not acquired the skill of tracking this data, therefore causing them never to know their true status as a student. Students assume that because they move from grade level to grade level, regardless of classes passed or credits earned, they are progressing forward. I was astonished at the number of students who were freshman seniors. Then, I realized that it was due mostly to students choosing their classes. As a result, they had all electives or classes they felt were easy for them to pass while bypassing mandated courses needed for graduation like mathematics, language arts, sciences, history/government, and electives. This is a major concern for many reasons but mainly because many are having their graduation completion date elongated.

Discipline

Once again, discipline is a major issue in inner-city schools, causing teachers to spend an enormous amount of time in redirection in lieu of teaching. I am not sure how this started nor where, but removing students from the classroom should not be a disciplinary action.

As a teacher, you are required to educate the students on your roster, and when you remove a student, it causes the student to miss out on important content needed for them to pass an assessment for that concept.

Parents, when this occurs, it is important that you inform your child or the teacher that you would like your child to have the notes or assignment he/she missed out on and that you would like to be contacted when your child misbehaves.

English Language Learners

If you have children who fall into this category, you must keep a close eye on services. Teachers who are servicing students who fall into this category should have a Structured English Immersion (SEI) endorsement or English as a Second Language (ESL) degree, and if you do not, what strategies are you using to assist students with their learning?

I am only asking because a lack of learning tools could lead to why students are struggling. Please understand this is not to stab at you for attempting to assist with the learning. When a student already has a barrier to their learning (language), then it's necessary for you to have the skills needed to assist or you're hindering the student's learning.

If you have a child who struggles with the English language, your assistance as the parent is greatly needed for your child for him/her to have the best education possible. Remember that teachers in the United States must instruct in English for every classroom that is not a foreign language class. With the state of Arizona removing their mandated English Language Learner program, which assists students with this language deficiency, it is up to the parent to now assist with strengthening the student's understanding of the language so the student has a greater opportunity at following along in the classroom. The best way to go about providing at-home assistance is through in-house tutoring or buying a program such as Babel to assist.

Even though schools purchase curriculums to support English language learning, students still need to be aware of the language to benefit from the curriculum. Again, this is where not doing homework elongates the learning. If you are partially using the curriculum because your school does not give homework, then the learning time is being extended drastically, causing many students to be unsuccessful in passing the Arizona English Language Learner Assessment (AZELLA).

Encouragement

Parents, this is a huge part of the student's learning. If the student does not feel encouraged to learn by participating in classroom discussions or activities, he/she may spend their entire day while at school doing nothing. Trust me; it is taking place daily. There are only so many bad grades that a student will take before giving up and feeling like school is just not for them. Unfortunately, when the student begins to feel this way, he/she becomes so bored with the lesson in the classroom, and he/she now begins to find ways to disrupt the learning. By instruction is interrupted, it causes a domino effect, and many other planned items for the lesson fall by the wayside. When the time the teacher manages to redirect the behavior in the classroom, the bell has rung and students have now been dismissed. However, when students are encouraged to do their best and to give 100 percent, they go all out to please you, the parent, and everyone else who believes in them.

Parents, I support you 100 percent, and the challenges you face while raising your children to be the best they can be while fighting society's pressures, finances, housing, safety, and anything else that complicates child-rearing.

Engagement

Parents, please make sure your child participates in the learning by answering questions and by asking questions. When students are not engaged, the teacher assumes that they understand and move on to the next task.

Many children come to school sleeping in the classroom or distracted by their cell phones during the lesson. That, coupled with a low interest in education, causes students to be disengaged entirely from activities or assignments given in the classroom.

Engagement in the lesson is part of the learning, and if your child is not engaged in the learning and he/she is not completing homework, then the child is not learning or progressing in their learning. Therefore, it is important to stay involved with your child's learning throughout the year.

Unfortunately, if your child is identified as a troublemaker by the school or teacher due to the number of consequences they have endured, many teachers will allow them to sleep in the classroom just as long as they do not disrupt the learning for others. At no time is this okay, but the teacher feels as though he/she has no help with preventing the child from sleeping, so the outcome is to let the student sleep.

This turns into a major issue because the child now believes they can disengage from learning anytime they do not want to participate. Word travels fast in a school setting, and before you know it, there are two to three other students following the same actions.

Effort still holds a lot of merit in the classroom. If students come to school and give their very best each and every time or attempt to do their best, they will always come out on top regarding passing the class.

Teachers are fully aware that concepts will be too difficult for some students to learn, due to the lack of skills they possess for understanding these concepts; however, when the student attempts to work with the teacher in small groups during class and on homework assignments, the teacher will remember the student's efforts during grading. This is not to say they will get an A for effort, nor should they, but they can get a legitimate passing grade.

Functional Illiteracy

According to the *Merriam-Webster Dictionary and Thesaurus*, a functional illiterate is a "person who has had some schooling but does not meet a minimum standard of literacy." Now I know this sounds unpleasant to hear, but if we, as parents, do not get more involved in our child's learning, this is what many inner-city graduates look like.

The reason functional illiteracy occurs is due to the following: students not doing homework or practicing the skill they learned, students sleeping during instruction, leaders not caring about the education of his/her students, schools operating without curricula or curricula that are not a good fit for the students they service, teachers not caring, students missing an overabundance of school seat time, students not reading, parents with little schooling, lack of books at home and lack of stimulation as to the importance of reading, and doing poorly at or dropping out of school. Many have not completed high school and have difficult living conditions, including poverty, learning disabilities, such as dyslexia, dysorthographia, etc.

Unfortunately, many parents are experiencing more than one of the items mentioned above. As a result, the child's opportunities are now limited. Avoiding functional illiteracy is imperative for school and families to work together. School libraries often provide families with free resources to assist with student learning. Please take advantage of this opportunity and work with the school on avoiding functional illiteracy from occurring with your child.

Reading is possibly the most important subject to learn, as it pertains to life. Lack of ability in this area affects job/career opportunities, communication, and livelihood.

General Education Degree

I chose this topic for the letter G based on the number of parents and students who say they will get a GED instead of dealing with the consequences that cause us to have this meeting. Yes, a GED is another option for demonstrating completion of required courses needed. However, even for a GED, the student still needs to complete the same courses they were attempting to avoid while attending the brick and mortar.

For some people, obtaining a GED will be even more challenging because you do not have someone in front of them, like a teacher, showing you the process needed for solving the concept. Now there are GED courses you can take that will prepare you for taking the test at the end of the course, but remember, passing the test is the final step needed for completion, and without a passing score on the test, the course is considered incomplete.

Acquiring a GED is different from acquiring a high school diploma. One must still complete the basic courses—science, mathematics, social studies, and language arts—in order to receive a GED. Each subject requires you to pass a test to demonstrate what you have retained.

Therefore, if you have trouble learning from someone else and test anxiety and you do not like sitting in class, taking notes, studying, or taking a test, acquiring a GED will not be as easy as it sounds.

Homework

Parents, please do not let anyone convince you that homework is not necessary because it is a scam, as they say. Homework is the reason someone gets better, if not great, at whatever they are doing. Regardless of the task, if it were not for repetitive practice, they would not have achieved success in that area.

For example, imagine a new reporter not practicing the use of proper English. We see it all the time. They are just not on the news. Imagine a professional athlete not preparing for the sport. We saw that as well when one of the greatest fighters ever lost his belt to the underdog, Douglas.

Understand that a teacher usually only has an hour to teach your child a standard. Whatever the student learned for that day, it should continue by completing homework. This format occurs in every class; therefore, it must be practiced to retain the amount of information learned.

Time after time, I have noticed students, during my observations or evaluations, feel as though they have a complete understanding of the work and do not need to participate anymore during the class. When I asked them the next day about class, they told me it was not easy.

Here is why many students again in the inner city feel as though they do not need to take notes during class because they were answering questions throughout the entire time, so they get it. The problem is, yes, you answered questions during class, but now you are at home without the teacher's guidance or anything to refer to because you did not take notes. It never fails. The student returns the next day and has to start learning over. This is a problem because it elongates the student's learning, forcing him/her to now learn two standards as the class moves on.

To fix this concern, the teacher needs to mandate note-taking, and hopefully, as the parent, you can enforce note-taking and inform your child that you will be checking to see if he/she took notes.

Individualized Educational Plan (IEP)

This term relates to special education. An individualized plan is developed by the parent, the special education team (which includes the teachers, coaches, special education director), and someone who acts as the Local Education Agency (LEA) or school administrator.

The purpose of the team is to prevent any decisions from being made by one person. The team must agree on what is needed for the child. Unfortunately, when we are *all* unaware of this rule, one may assume they can dictate the direction, but that is not true.

Once developed, it should outline the disability, deficiencies caused by the disability, and the amount of assistance provided, identified in minutes, to help your child with the learning. The special education program is to *help* the child, not harm the child.

The only way a child in special education should ever receive an F is if the child refuses to do the work and it was not outlined in the IEP as an option. Students identified should be graded on the progress they are making toward their goal as stated in the IEP and not on their ability to complete their work.

Every three years, the plan should be reevaluated, if not rewritten. During this time, you as the parent, should be tracking the minutes provided to ensure your child receives the amount of assistance needed for the learning as deemed in the IEP.

Joking

I thought this was important because of the number of cases I had to deal with as an administrator when one student jokes and the other one does not. Joking seems to have reached an all-time high in this era we live today, the twenty-first century. However, playing with the wrong person today, preferably inside or outside the classroom, could be deadly.

Students thrive off reputation, so embarrassing them with a joke or prank means that you tainted their reputation, and the only way to counter that is to protect themselves however they see fit. With this mindset, it often leads to fights or worse.

Anytime society presents more violence than assimilation, students believe this is the way they need to behave in order to survive.

Keep in Touch

Parents, if you have a hard time communicating with the school due to such a hectic work schedule, I have devised something that I have been using for years, and parents love it. It's based on written communication and involves the teacher, parent, and student.

I used this form for behavior and academics. I developed the idea back in 2003 for a parent who did not have the time to talk but wanted to be more involved with her child's education. This form allowed us to discuss day-to-day activities as well as work completed for the day. Truly, it is a daily monitoring system for the parent.

I know many schools have a parent portal, and I know it's easy, but for me, as an educator with children in school, I would prefer to read something instead of opening an app or using some form of technology. Yes, I still prefer to read the Sunday paper and not gather my information from the internet.

Lunch

Attending school with free and reduced lunch means that the school resides in a low economic status environment causing the school to have a government-funded lunch program. Food options are not always what students prefer, but it is still important and healthy for the student to eat. Unfortunately, students are going days without eating lunch because they do not like the choices offered.

Please remember that food is nourishment, so when the student does not eat, it drains their energy, causing them to not have the endurance needed for shuffling through a seven-hour day. In most cases, when the student does not eat, he/she gets irritable, and that frustration bleeds into the classroom, causing further issues. Government-funded lunch programs are regulated, causing food selections to be limited; however, they *all* offer a drink, fruit, and various types of meat (e.g., lunch meat, chicken, hot dogs, or pizza with pepperoni).

Please encourage your child to eat something during the day to assist them in having a productive day. Playing sports during lunch instead of eating causes the body to seek other ways of replenishing the energy it would have gotten from foods needed for the body to operate correctly.

Mathematics

Parents do not let people convince you that learning algebra or mathematics in school is a waste of time! This is probably the biggest myth ever made about education. Now I admit, you may not need mathematics for all occupations, but you still apply mathematics outside of your daily job, and here is how. To avoid asking for assistance, you must know what you learned in math to determine the balance. An algebraic equation would be the most available equation to apply.

Algebra exists in everyday life, and when one uses it, they probably do not realize it because they were not in a school setting. Anytime you can merge outside learning with the content learned in school, you have a better understanding of that concept and why it is recommended for you to know.

Can you imagine the following professions not knowing mathematics? Carpenter, architect, engineer, home builder, tax preparer, landscaper, construction worker, electricians, and so on... Just because you feel you do not use it does not mean it is not important. It means you are in a field of choice that does not require mathematics but that does not hold any merit regarding other occupations. Learning mathematics is just as vital as reading.

Numbers

Parents, when teachers or the school cannot get in touch with you to notify you about your child, it becomes a real problem. I understand that you do not want teachers calling you at your job every time your child does something wrong.

I would like to suggest either using another method or arranging a time with the teacher to discuss updates or concerns. I am saying this because it is so frustrating as an administrator when we need to reach someone and can't and it is due to an emergency. Please make sure the school has the correct contact information to reach you for of your child's well-being. Refer back to keep in touch for ideas if needed.

Online Learning

This new process has wholly diminished the purpose of school. Instead of there being feuding between charter and public, educators should be more concerned with online learning programs educating our youth. The more successful this program becomes, the fewer schools need you as a teacher.

Online learning programs are no different from automated programs taking over employee jobs, as both are computer based. The problem with online learning is that every student is not an online learner and online school programs do not have someone on standby waiting for you to ask them a question. Sure, there may be a way you can get your item (s) addressed, but will it be prompt enough?

When a student attends school, they not only learn concepts of various subjects, but they also develop their character, social skills, communication skills, collaboration, and possibly a better understanding of right and wrong from interactions with their peers.

If you are still not convinced, here another way to view this. Although some stores offer amazing discount prices, some items are worth paying full price. Otherwise, get what you pay for.

Phone Calls

Parents, I know that you get tired of teachers calling you regarding something negative about your child. I get it. However, here are two suggestions I beg you to consider.

1. If multiple teachers call you within the same week about something your child may have done, chances are it is true. I say this because teachers do not like making hostile phone calls, especially when there is a high probability that they will be cursed out, so if they chose to take the risk and call you, I would say it is probably true.
2. The second suggestion is, if the teacher did not call you the day before to discuss your child's behavior and he/she did not call you the week early to discuss anything negative about your child, then, as an administrator and former teacher, I would say the reason they are calling is to acquire your assistance with something wrong that involves your child.

If you encounter any of the following, please communicate peacefully and respectfully to resolve the issue. When the conversation is not polite, the student realizes that he/she can play you against one another and may use that strategy to get out of trouble. Believe it or not, the student even comes to school to brag about how he/she played you guys against one another, and the battle now appears to be between the parent and the teacher as the child watches, listens, and eat popcorn during the show.

Quality Time

Parents, I know this may seem a little traditional and times have changed since we were all on the same page regarding education, but if you could just make sure your child spends some quality time learning, I promise you that you will see a world of difference in their academics.

There used to be a time when we believed that when the child gets home from school, he/she is expected to study at the kitchen table for the next hour or however long it takes to complete their homework. I believe this belief has diminished over time because today, students seem to have an array of study habits that works for them.

I started recognizing the various study habits in college and it is the same today. For example, many students study today with music blasting, while eating, with the noise surrounding them, while working on something else, or even while watching television.

The problem we have is children using strategies for studying without actually studying, and that has to stop in order to make a difference. Sometimes students feel the joke is on the teacher because they are assuming they are getting away with not doing their work, but the joke is actually on them. They just won't realize it until later in life.

If it's not broken, do not attempt to fix it, but if it's broken, change it.

Quadrilateral

As we know, this is a geometrical shape, and I use this to help parents when they have a hard time keeping up with their child's academics. This is a temporary solution that can become permanent if needed. The four sides to focus on are reading for fifteen minutes, take notes for fifteen minutes, answer questions, and study for fifteen minutes daily, and your child will begin to see academic results.

Reading

As you all know, our children are reflections of who we are. If students see that reading is important to you because they watch you read the newspaper every day or your favorite magazine when you get home, they, too, will view reading as necessary.

Even if you do not have the time to read to them, have them read to you. Even high school students get excited about reading aloud. Students should read for at least thirty minutes a day until they have increased their level of reading and comprehension.

While working with your child on expanding their reading skills, it is vital that he/she chooses reading material that will allow them to read fluently. The more students struggle when reading, causing them to stop reading or pause because every other word is too difficult for them, the easier it will be for them to shut down from reading.

Reading should be a natural occurrence where one can read with fluency while acknowledging punctuation marks within the reading. Students in junior high through high school should read for at least an hour a day. This task should seem seamless since there are twenty-four hours in a day, and you do not have to read for an hour straight, although you will increase your reading endurance by increasing your reading time.

Reading should entail proper pronunciation of consonant and vowel sounds, fluency, expression, comprehension, and recall. Parents, if your child follows the following components to reading daily, I promise their reading level and understanding will increase.

With the work schedule that many parents in the inner city face today, it isn't easy to sometimes ensure that occurs. If you fall into that situation as a parent and want the best for your child, but time is not on your side, here are a few tips to assist your child with his/her reading skills.

Step one. Chose a book that your child can read with confidence. Even if the book appears to be too easy, that is okay. Our first goal is to get them reading consistently. This is easier to do when they enjoy the content. As for now, it does not really matter what they are reading for entertainment as long as it is appropriate and meets your guidelines as a parent.

Step two. Create a time when reading can occur daily. If possible, chose a time when you can be there, but if that is not possible, select a time for them to read and try to make it the same time every day. With the child reading every day at the same time, it will begin to help the child develop a schedule.

Step three. Make the reading mandatory. This means that the child should be able to demonstrate to you that they did their homework. In 2020, technology makes this step extremely simple. As a parent, you need to verify the reading, and here are a few ways to determine completion:

a) The lesson can be recorded and left for you to hear when you come home.
b) A summary can be left for you, explaining what the reading was about.
c) Text notes to you.
d) You can communicate with your child about the reading when you return.

Each component of step three will help enhance the other. The most important thing is that reading occurs and it can be proven.

Step four. As a teacher and administrator, I have always said that a student's writing skills should be equal to his/her reading skills. Writing should be practiced just as much as reading, especially if you have aspirations for your child to go to college.

There are too many schools stating they are following College and Career Readiness Standards but writing is not a focus. Students must prepare for college, and writing happens to be one of the most essential subjects in college since you have to write in every class (e.g., science labs, math word problems, or explaining concepts in written form, history reports, and the list goes on).

If all else fails, use this guide for making sure your child completes their daily reading

Reading Schedule/Planner

Day of the Week	Number of Pages	Story or Content	Length of Time	Concept of Story
Monday				
Tuesday				
Wednesday				
Thursday				
Friday				

If children use this planner daily with diligence, they will begin to see the efficiency of their reading.

When children fail reading assessments given to them in school, their reading endurance is not long enough to withstand the amount of reading associated with the question and they struggle with the vocabulary. As they begin to read more, they will enhance their vocabulary skills and understanding of the author's purpose.

Respect

Without mutual respect, learning is complicated for the child and all others in the classroom. When there is no concern for one another's well-being, the smallest disruptions and misunderstandings will lead to significant classroom disorders.

Here is a fact. When a student who is not known for cursing or disrespecting the teacher, and is around other students with no regard for the consequences, the respectful student begins to think it's standard and slowly starts to show signs of disrespect themselves by cursing during class or speaking negatively to the teacher.

When learning is the focus, respect is given from both sides without anyone feeling the need to earn it. Often, I hear students saying the teacher needs to achieve their care, and I would reply by saying they earned it already by getting up in the morning to educate you. Look around you.

How many other people do you see taking on the available position or opportunity to do the same?

Social Media

Who knew this would become an avenue for negativity instead of positive interaction? Social media is our new form of bullying in 2020. Students are dehumanized through social media, and it normally spills over into the school system.

Students are discovering so many ways to hide their social media platforms. Even if you monitor your child's use, it is still hard to identify, allowing them to discuss or partake in things that would normally be forbidden, can be costly.

Regardless of the popularity of social media and the popularity of peers, I still believe that parents are the most substantial influence to children, and if you are involved in your child's life, by communicating with them and ensuring they are honest with you, social media should not out-shadow your parenting.

Special Education

Let me begin by saying this is a federal law, and student services are mandated. Parents, this is not a harmful component to your child's education. It is designed to support your child's education. If diagnosed as someone who needs this program for their academic development, it is imperative that you ensure the assistance is being provided for the benefit of your child.

Knowing the law associated with special education offers a better opportunity for you and the school to collaborate on what's best and needed for the child's education. Positive communication will enhance services being provided for the child at school and possibly at home.

Parents, be aware and mindful of FERPA. Remember, this law allows students to govern their own education by making all educational decisions once they turn eighteen. Unfortunately, due to student's distaste for the special education program, they view it as more of a handicap than assistance and decide to withdraw from the program without knowing what all comes along with that decision.

When a child withdraws from the SPED program due to FERPA laws, they no longer need assistance to complete the required work. This also means that now the school cannot communicate with the parents for any further assistance. As a parent, I am concerned because the student doesn't know the law pertaining to special education and could damage themselves from meeting graduation requirements.

Once your child joins the special education program, their academic learning should be guided by the Individualized Educational Plan. Growth in the child's learning comes from meeting goals established within the IEP, and that is what should be graded by teachers.

Time Management

Parents, if your child uses an excuse as to why they did not get something done such as homework or chores, it is not because they ran out of time but because they do not know how to manage their time. This is not as easy as it sounds, and as your responsibility increases, your time to accomplish your task will seem to decrease.

Once students learn how to manage their time; they will see that they have more time on their hands than they bargained on. Training children to work off a schedule helps the child become more studious and assists with responsibilities outside the home and prepares them for the workforce upon graduating from high schools.

Unity

Unless we come together as a community school and demonstrate why students benefit from attending a brick and mortar, parents and students will explore other methods for their schooling. Right now, the only thing holding this hypothesis back from being proven correctly is finances, but when this is figured out, the art of teaching will be in jeopardy.

Value

The value of school and a good education starts with your parenting. If children know that you value school and good education, they will do what is necessary to get the job done even if they do not enjoy the workload that comes with learning.

The more we allow children to assume education is not important; the attrition rates will continue to rise. It is our responsibility to provide children with all the tools needed to be academically successful, and when we do not, we play an important role in the outcome. The lack of value leads to a lack of performance, participation, and planning for the future. As stated before, if you fail to plan, you plan to fail.

Worksheets

The purpose of a worksheet is to allow the student time to practice whatever concept they learned during class. The worksheet should cover enough problems to determine if the student clearly understands the standard. Practice should be an enjoyable process that does not lead to frustration and anger because the student cannot perform the task at hand.

Also, just because the child does not have a worksheet, it does not mean that the child does not have homework. This seems to be a misleading myth, causing so many students to fall behind. You do not need a worksheet to practice reading or math problems learned during class.

When students develop their problems, they are said to have a more complex understanding of what was taught.

(X—Not applicable to this reading)

Your Turn

Parents, please take this opportunity to show that you are willing to work with the school collaboration in providing your child with the best education possible. This is all about setting your child up for success, and I know you want that.

I would like to guarantee you that if your child sees that you are willing to work with the school in a joint effort to educate them, you will begin to see your child flourish in their academic ability.

Arizona Zip Code Project

This was an excellent opportunity for people in the community, and I hope there is a chance to reestablish these people. I enjoyed working with some fantastic leaders who helped show members of the community they care—First Institutional Church, Robison's Law Firm, Drop Out Recovery Program (DRP), Teen First, Accord, and many others.

*****

Teachers, I hope this section of the book serves its intended purpose. I want you to know before going any further that I believe you have one of the most critical occupations in the world today. Even though it may not be as valued by others once success levels have been reached, I wonder if any of those opposed would have reached that success without education.

The challenges that you encounter daily for which you continue to strive for the best, says a lot about your heart and character. I hope that our profession will be as valued financially as some of the other occupations that weigh heavily on that person having a sound education.

I am writing to you to share some of the strategies I used inside and outside the classroom. Please understand that the items I will discuss only assist you as a teacher and hopefully provide a few tools with any items you may be struggling within the classroom.

Below is a list of terms used to help me deliver the information I would like to share with you. While reviewing the information below, please know that not all terms pertain to you, or you may not need assistance at all, but if it's useful to you, then please enjoy it.

At the end of this book will be my contact information in case I need to elaborate further for clarification. I hope this will be beneficial as you prepare for yet another style of teaching due to COVID-19. Be blessed and stay safe.

Attire

Teachers, I know times are difficult right now, especially during this pandemic, but I want to take the time to share with you from an administrator's position about school dress code. It may not appear to be a priority, but trust me when I tell you that it has a greater impact than you think.

When I was attending school as a student, the teacher's attire demonstrated to students the respect teachers had for the position. My friends and I still discuss some of the teacher's attire when drifting back to school topics. As a student, it was impressive to see the attire of a profession that was different than what we were surrounded by growing up, which were factory uniforms for most of our parents. Therefore, seeing teachers in shirts and ties meant you were important and was seen as a leader.

Even though this was still considered a blue-collar position, it carried the merit of respect. When teachers dressed down for the day, they still wore clothes that demonstrated the difference between students and instructors.

Today in 2020, dress down is every day, and there are times when you cannot tell the difference between the teacher and student from afar. If you want students to respect you and follow what you say, you must demonstrate to them that you also respect the position you were hired to do.

Try viewing it this way. When you want to impress someone, maybe on a first date or so, don't you dress to the best of your ability? I am assuming you are doing that because you want to make a

33

statement about who you are and how you feel about the person you are meeting. If you carry that same belief into your classroom, your students will begin to view you differently. If you carry that belief throughout the year, your students will begin to know that you are there to share with them, and they will begin to appreciate your time.

As an administrator, I made an attempt to wear a shirt and tie every day, and on the days I did not, I made sure I was sharply dressed. When someone came into my school, they may not have known who I was, but they quickly gathered I was someone of importance based on how I was dressed compared to everyone else.

My attire also aided me as an administrator in dealing with parents because it commanded respect but not in a negative way. Usually, people associate a shirt and tie as someone who should assist them with their concern, and I was always happy to accept the challenge.

Your students will show you the same courtesy if you show them the benefit of wearing proper clothing during school. I say "during school" because sometimes we, as educators, get confused with parenting versus educating. Our goal is not to change or insult their clothing choices but to guide them to self-respect and the impacts of appearance.

As a new teacher coming into a profession in which you are only five (or less) years older than the audience you are teaching, this will really help with managing the classroom. When you dress like the students, you are altering the level of respect you should want as the classroom leader. Dressing like students do not make students feel as though you are in tune with their generation. In fact, students need someone to look up to, not horizontally.

In 2018, as an administrator, I remember another administrator asking me why I wore a shirt and tie every day. I informed him because I was ecstatic about what I do and wanted it to show in my attire. He replied that he stopped doing it because it made his parents feel uncomfortable. I stated to myself that if they are uncomfortable, it is probably not due to your clothing. Most parents that I had worked with appreciated the fact that the leader of their child's school has pride in himself/herself as well as what he/she does.

Believe it or not; students also enjoy dressing up. I held an event for students to dress up annually, and at the end, they would always ask me when they can do it again.

One of my biggest events was Ladies' Day. No matter what school I attended, I implemented this program. I would make it a huge event and would promote it for at least two months to show its importance. As students arrived, I would gather them in the auditorium where we had a movie in their honor set up. Last year it was *Hidden Figures*. As the ladies watched a movie, the men would prepare lunch for the day. When the movie ended, students were escorted to the auditorium, decorated in their honor. Next, the men served lunch, and each male staff member and student who wanted to give a two-minute speech about the positive impact women have made on their life would speak about it. The ladies received a rose, and we recorded the event to always display during school.

The way you dress can dictate the atmosphere of the environment you are in. Why not make the best of it?

Assessments

I know this is a touchy subject, but it must be covered. Teachers, here is why assessments are so important. As an administrator, we have to report data to so many resources that use the data we collect for them to determine our effectiveness as a school.

Yes, there are other components used to determine success levels, but you are not operating based on those components. You are operating because you were approved to educate students based on the plan that you presented.

Therefore, as a check and balance system, assessment data displays if you are doing what you said you were going to do. People say that standardized assessments should not be given—that they are culturally biased; they do not determine overall knowledge, test anxiety, and many others. The truth is, assessments only assess what you should have learned. If students are not learning in your classroom, then that must be addressed. I do not understand why this is a problem for so many educators. It would be best if you welcomed the opportunity of someone helping you fine-tune your skills.

To help students be comfortable with assessments, refer to quizzes. Students need to feel comfortable about assessments before caring about them. If students have constantly failed assessments, they may believe this is something they cannot achieve and give up on it. To change that mindset, provide small quizzes that cover five questions or less on items covered during the week. After monitoring student growth for several quizzes, you can determine if you would like to increase the questions. This strategy works well when you have to differentiate the learning.

Attendance

This seems to be very difficult to complete with fidelity, as they say. Attendance plays a major role with finances. When you are late taking your attendance or forget to take it, it creates unnecessary adjustments that need to be made for the student and school. At times, it causes a problem with how your school may have been funded. Whatever you do, please adhere to the importance of taking attendance because it affects not only you but also others.

Benchmark Assessments

It is important that you have benchmark assessments to determine your effectiveness as an instructional leader. Benchmark assessments should be used as a guide to identifying how close you are to being successful when taking the state assessment.

Benchmarks should be given at least three times a year. Make sure your assessment tool asks the same style of questions that students will see on the summative assessment at the end of the year. When assessments are not aligned, students have difficulty adjusting.

Since benchmark assessments are not frequently given; I still suggest that you provide minute quizzes throughout the duration to get students back into testing mode. Students get out of test mode because they are not used to taking assessments, or they do not have the stamina for their assessments.

Testing should come naturally to students. Unfortunately, many people assume that too much testing is causing students to become unsuccessful, and that could not be further from the truth. Too much non purposeful testing can create boredom, but when students expect assessments and have been properly prepared, they anxiously wait to see the outcome.

Black Lives Matter

My heart and prayers go out to Floyd's family, and thank goodness justice prevailed, but the fight is not over. This negative behavior must come to a close in all aspects of life, even in education. If we learn how to treat people with respect, we can cover so much more ground. As it pertains to the classroom teachers, please understand the importance of celebrating Black History Month. It baffles me when I have to remind teachers to honor this month and what's worse is that some Black teachers are not honoring this month.

Teachers, if you want to have a rapport with your minority students, show them how you have respect for who they are, especially during a month that honors their race. Society often demonstrates racism in the worst way, so you must show the difference between what takes place outside the classroom and what you allow inside the classroom. You fight visual negativity with visual positivity. It's okay to discuss the world's wrongdoings, but be sure to show them the other side to the coin.

For teachers out there who are not interested in honoring Black History Month even though you have Black students in the classroom, please adhere to the effect your decision has on students. When I talked to teachers about this concern, they mostly stated how bored they had become with the redundancy of promoting the same African Americans year after year. I have the utmost respect to all our forefathers who have paved the way for our people, but we can diversify whom we learn about and how we learn about them in 2020.

Book reports are nice, but technology has advanced so much since book reports were considered the best way to display what you have learned. Explore all opportunities for creativity with students. If we get back to focusing on the learning, more students will shine if given opportunities to demonstrate their individuality.

Block Scheduling

I am not sure why so many schools, mostly charter, have gravitated to this schedule, but it serves as a disservice to students when schools do not supply teachers with the materials that should accompany the learning for this length of time. If you are failing and this is your schedule, this could serve as a major reason why you are underperforming.

Block scheduling was designed to provide two different types of learning in one classroom session. Normally, block scheduling has traditional learning followed by a constructivist style of learning. However, when teachers are not given the additional materials to support the curriculum, schools force teachers to become lecturers without the proper audience for lecturing.

For block scheduling to be effective, you have to have a teacher who is familiar with both styles of delivery—traditional and constructivist—as well as someone who can plan for this amount of time to be useful and purposeful. This is not easy but when done correctly, it's impactful.

Unfortunately, block scheduling causes teachers to spend hours and hours on elongated lesson plans. If you know as a teacher that Johnny cannot sit for ninety minutes without making a distraction because his attention span is not that long, then be proactive in your planning to prepare for those distractions. When in team meetings and you discover that other teachers are experiencing the same concerns, trust me, your schedule is only part of the issue.

If you must have block scheduling, then create an opportunity for students to relearn some of those foundational skills they lost along the way to increase learning and student performance. You will find this strategy to serve as better use of that blocked time.

Chunking

Teachers, if you are struggling with students in your classroom learning the concept and keeping up with the note-taking that is required, it is because you are giving them too much information to process.

Learning should be a gradual process. Although some people may learn faster than others, if your students are underperforming, they would benefit from a slower delivery.

By chunking information that you want the students to retain, you give them a chance to process, relate and place that information in their long-term memory until it is needed.

Classroom Management

In 2020, this word is so archaic that it should be placed into the museum of education. Classroom management has no effect when students disrupt learning with no consequences. If teachers cannot manage the classroom because the administration cannot manage the school, then the school should probably develop an Effective Management Plan (EMP).

This process levels the playing field for *all* participants and places everyone on the same accord by holding *all* responsible for their actions. An EMP would eliminate 80–90 percent of low-level classroom disruptions.

The problem with classroom management is that everyone has a different form of use, causing some students to behave in some rooms while others are chaotic. Individualized rules pertaining to a school cause massive confusion for students going from one class to another. Believe it or not, classroom management also causes students to favor one teacher over the other one due to the classroom rules and procedures applied. When learning is the focus of the school, everything else falls in to place, causing classroom management to be the last of your concerns.

Cultural Differences

Cultural differences can have a major impact on the learning of your students. When the relationships among races are not positive in society, the same reasons for why this occurs enters the classroom. This is not to say that we cannot learn from one another, but students must be able to trust the person they are following. Students can determine how much you care about the learning and the students from the environment of the classroom and your interaction with them. If students do not feel a positive vibe because you never interact with them or if the only time you speak to them is when you are yelling at them, they will dislike you and assume that you do not like minorities. You can say whatever you want, but your actions will tell the true story.

For example, if you allow students to curse in the classroom and then write them up for cursing because you were already in a bad mood, that is going to have a negative impact on how students feel about you.

Also, you cannot buy students' love. By this, you cannot assume that because you allow students to play games, they are going to like or respect you. The moment the games go away, reality sets in.

Once again, focus on learning. Students know they are in an underperforming school or district, and they also know that the games you allow them to play will not advance their learning in any way. Basically, you are making them think you do not really care.

Critical Thinking

As educators, if we ever want to close the achievement gap, we must get our students to reach certain level of thinking on a daily basis. You can't expect students to think critically when questions do not entail a depth of understanding. For example, I do not have to think critically about true-false questions, it is either T or F.

Critical thinking requires the teacher to change his/her questioning techniques. Questions should now be more open-ended, allowing the students to discover the answer. Although it has been rewritten with a visual to make it appear new, Bloom's taxonomy is still considered the best way to get students to use their critical thinking skills.

When using Bloom's taxonomy, it is important to know that the first two levels require no higher-order thinking. This style of questions are more or less good for bell work, Q and A in the classroom, or when learning vocabulary.

The strength of critical thinking comes from the planning. A methodical plan of execution for getting students to use their critical thinking skills must come from having the end in mind when planning. This strategy allows you to ensure that all activities lead to the end goal.

As you strengthen students' way of thinking, you should gradually move them to the next level of Bloom's taxonomy. Unlike other thinking methods, Bloom's taxonomy is sequential and should be learned one level at a time. At one time, it was said that students should never reach the highest level of Bloom's taxonomy; however, that has changed with the creativeness of our youth.

Webb's "Depth of Knowledge" Wheel is also a good tool for getting students to think on a higher level, and it is not sequential, meaning you can interchange between the levels while learning.

Covert Reading

This is not a good activity when it is not followed by an overt activity. Telling students to read without checking to see if they did read is just saying to students, "You need a break." When doing choral reading activities, everyone should be reading the same content to challenge students' comprehension.

When students are underperforming, reading needs to be purposeful. Yes, pleasure reading is a relaxing activity but should not overshadow the curriculum. Students must learn how to read from the content being used to guide their instruction.

Compliance versus Caring

Sometimes the pressures of not doing so well academically forces teachers to move into compliance in lieu of caring. For example, teachers have a habit of moving through standards even if students do not understand the concepts. This rapid pace of covering multiple standards as quickly as possible causes students to fall behind. As students move from standard to standard without learning, instructions serves no purpose.

Yes, the students play a role in their failing status, but I am referring to what we could be prevented if compliance was not leading the drive. I know there are times when you have no control—and I get it—but when you can control the pace and the learning, show students how much you care by slowing down and ensuring that students are retaining what is being taught.

When students see that you refuse to let them fail, they will have more respect for you than you can imagine. Inner-city students have encountered many adults who have given up on them, but they do not often embrace adults who hang in there with them till the end. This belief has always worked in my favor, causing me to have an amazing rapport with students and teachers. Often, people tell me I cannot speak about education without showing my passion. I just like to say I care.

Clutter

Teachers, please make sure that your room is not cluttered and that students are able to be mobile if the lesson requires for movement. If you are not using it, remove it from your room. If you do not, you will become a hoarder, assuming that you use everything in the room, even the material with the cobwebs. I stress the importance of clutter because some students who are living in poverty never experience cleanliness due to the number of children in the home, lack of domesticated family members at home, or lack of finances, which causes for the limited furniture or storage which aids in cleanliness.

Remember: the rules for a good testing environment should be the rules for everyday learning.

Constructive Criticism

Tension is so high when you are in an underperforming school that most advice given to the teachers is taken as a negative feedback or insult to their performance. Usually this belief occurs when the teacher fears losing their job due to concerns of administration. Teachers should not have to fear losing a job due to not performing a task correctly. They should be able to receive assistance that would correct the concern. Unfortunately, when you are under a dictatorship, the leader is not knowledgeable enough to assist in your classroom, so they blame you for those imperfections instead.

Constructive criticism should lead to positive dialogue between the teacher and the person who has the concern. This process strengthens the teacher's confidence in knowing they can now collaborate with its leader to improve their profession.

Data

Data should serve as the most used resource on your campus daily. Teachers, if you use the data to drive your instruction, you will begin to see academic growth. Unfortunately, many of us review our data and use it for compliance requests, but analyzing our data means using it to better the previous data obtained.

It is probably easier to name the items in schools that do not use data than to identify all that do. Data is used in the simplest form, such as determining the number of mopheads needed to clean the school, and the more complex forms, such as the formulas used to assess school letter grades.

Students should also be familiar with data and how to track data, as it pertains to their academic performance. There are too many students unfamiliar with the data used to determine their grade point average, letter grade, and semester grades. As students inspire to attend college, they should be familiar with how each item is calculated.

When students are familiar with what they need to do in order to reach a better academic score, they tend to apply more effort in achieving that goal. Hold students accountable for tracking assessment scores, and you can have students refer to their own data for questions concerning their letter grade.

Differentiation

I know this used to be the most complicated academic strategy for teachers to grasp. Still, with the pandemic in place, I am sure many of you get a clear understanding of how and why differentiation is a must for the classroom.

There used to be a time where schools would track students based on their grades, but that has been banned for decades; however, tracking students for subjects such as mathematics may not be a bad idea if you are trying to increase scores.

While doing observations as an administrator, I noticed that teachers struggled mostly with maintaining focus on the whole group while working in small groups with struggling students. Differentiation should not be provided when you have not assessed knowledge retained by students unless you have subgroups in your classroom and you already know differentiation will be needed.

Differentiation should begin with your planning. This method allows you to be proactive when preparing for how you would like instruction to be delivered. If your classroom operates the same on most days due to students following the room's procedures, it would be wise for you to have a small group area already established for smoother transition times.

Do not let the word *differ* in differentiation fool you. When applying differentiation to your lessons, please understand that *all* students should initially hear the content simultaneously, and through teacher observation and formative assessments, differentiation should be applied.

For example, the whole class may be working on two-digit multiplication while more advanced learners are working on two-digit expansion with decimals. You must stay on the same concept with everyone or find yourself attempting to cover multiple standards. The concept is two-digit multiplication and enriched learning is added, decimals.

Eliciting for Participation

If a student does not participate in the classroom at no time, how do you evaluate that student? Underperforming means *all* students should be engaged in every lesson. This strategy should not be a negotiation. There are far too many students not participating during the classroom discussion. If a student does not participate even after being asked to join the classroom discussion, there is probably a reason why, and you should talk to that student to determine why they choose not to be engaged.

Most students like to demonstrate their intelligence level to their peers, but if the classroom environment is not welcoming, they will not risk being embarrassed by getting the question wrong. To change this behavior, you have to build the confidence of the student.

Students should not fear answering questions incorrectly during class. It should be part of the growing process, but if this belief has not been established, I guarantee you that it is a major reason for why students do not participate during classroom discussions.

English Language Proficiency Standards (ELP)

If you are teaching students in this category without utilizing the tools proven to be effective, it could be the reason why students in this sub group are struggling to be academically successful in your classroom.

Since the state of Arizona has removed the four-hour block schedule for identified ELL students to learn English, it is up to *all* teachers to assist students with learning the English language. This is not just the job of the language arts teacher; however, the language arts teacher should be providing other teachers language arts strategies that could assist with their subject area. In conjunction with Structured English Immersion (SEI) strategies, the ELP standards, aligned with state standards, should provide the assistance needed for ELL students to perform successfully.

Unfortunately, if you are teaching students in this category and are not familiar with any of the strategies listed above, you could be hindering your students' progress. You can only teach effectively what you know.

Evaluations

Teachers, I understand the need to get a good evaluation. Still, you have to agree that if most of your students in your classes fail, you cannot expect to receive an evaluation that identifies you as highly effective.

If we put our own concerns in front of the concerns of our students, then we are not considered to be student led. It is a double standard when students receive an F for underperforming but you receive a passing score on your evaluation for underperforming in your list of responsibilities.

As I stated many times throughout this dialogue, everyone will benefit if you focus on the learning. Focusing on the learning will elevate your planning, delivery, and follow through which are all the main components of an effective evaluation.

Whatever evaluation tool your school or district is using, familiarize yourself with its components so you can learn how to receive an effective score on your evaluation. Here is a tip I would always give my employees during our pre-evaluation conference. If you want to receive a high score on your evaluation, implement the components in a column that has the highest ranking. Most evaluation tools use a rubric format for measuring. Follow the clues in the column that will give you the highest score for that section.

You cannot present strategies from the rubric's underperforming column, but expect to receive scores from the effective column or higher. Far too often, I have had conversations with teachers and even disagreements with them regarding their score.

Evaluations are based on what the evaluator witness when they are visiting the classroom at that time. The evaluator should not base your scores on what they thought you meant or on what you may have done in the classroom prior to the evaluation.

Evaluations should be used to build teachers up, not tear them down. An evaluation should provide strategies to improve the performance of the teacher.

Teachers, if you receive a low score in any area of your evaluation, here is a tip to assist you: ask for help from your administrator. By asking your principal for assistance in this area, you show him/her that you want to do better and are willing to take the guidance needed for improvement.

Now, the deficiency you received on your evaluation is an area of concern for the school as well as you, the teacher. This is not an attack on the principal. In fact, it is the responsibility of the principal. As the leader of the school, the administrator's main job is to provide teachers with the tools needed for them to be successful inside the classroom. If that is not occurring, how is the principal helping to ensure their effectiveness?

When schools have a positive culture, everyone is willing to help one another so the school can shine as a whole. Education is based on levels of leadership. For example, the teacher's main role is to care for the students, the principal's main role is to assist the teachers. The superintendent's role and many others are to assist the principals with running an effective school. When any one of these links to the chain is broken, it causes a domino effect in which no one wants to be responsible for the damage.

Fundamentals

Teachers, let me be clear. When the content that is being learned is sequential in order for the student to proceed to the next level, you cannot bypass it and wonder why the students are not doing well. Many of us are teaching standards that students are not ready for because they didn't complete the fundamental stages that would have prepared them for the next level.

Yes, you do have standards to cover, and yes, students should be on grade level, but they are not; therefore, if you really want your students to be successful, it is a must that you find a way to embed those foundational skills with the current learning that is taking place. There are multiple ways for you to accomplish this:

a) Homework
b) Bell work
c) Exit tickets out the door
d) Downtime activities in the classroom
e) Pop quizzes

If you are in a block schedule, you have more than enough time to develop missing skills for students to be academically successful. Instead of giving students detentions, create opportunities for students to work on these skills. It always amazes me how educators feel they could bypass grade levels and expect students to understand the current standards they are working on. Teachers, if you follow these simple rules of developing missing skills, you will be amazed at the outcome. Together, we can make a positive difference in student performance but only by telling truth. Students are already aware of their current state, but if you make them feel that they can be successful without learning, then we are purposely setting them up for failure.

Grades

I know this is a touchy subject, but it must be discussed. As educators, we are constantly attempting to find ways to make the class easier for the student to be academically successful, but giving the Christmas grades in October, January, March, and May is hindering the student in more ways than you can imagine.

For example, I remember, as an administrator, teachers giving a student straight As because she worked hard in school, she did not curse during class, she always assisted the teacher when no one else would, and she completed most of her assignments.

As a result, she ended up with a 4.0 grade point average and received a scholarship for attending an instate school. Unfortunately, the day she found out about the scholarship, I was at a meeting and did not hear the news until the next day. When I arrived to work early that morning, I found a note that was left for me on my desk. The note was a simple message with eight or fewer words, and four of the words were misspelled.

My point is, if you have students who are inspired to attend college, which is *awesome*, then prepare them properly. Students who attend college, better be prepared to do a lot of writing, reading, calculating, and much more. Tell them that college is a step above high school and they need to be ready for that. I understand that we are not purposely trying to make students fail, but if we foresee what could occur based on our experience with college and the knowledge we have of the student, then it is our job to guide them correctly.

Homework

I tried not to cover the same topics with parents as I do with teachers but this is *very important*. Students must complete homework to get better. I remember a superintendent telling me homework was a waste of time, yet she has a Ph.D. I wonder if she completed that degree without doing homework.

I do not care who is doing the homework because if the student is watching the work being done, that is enough for me. As a teacher, you can make up the difference. What colleges are you informing students to attend that do not provide homework to their students? Homework provides the students the additional time needed to understand the concept.

If students do not practice what they are learning, how can they get better at it?

Intervention

Teachers, please know that intervention should only be applied to students who do not understand the traditional method for completing their assignment. When you apply intervention for someone who already understands the concept, you are basically wasting the student's time. Now that the student is bored and need something to do, here comes the classroom disruptions.

If you are worried about keeping everyone on the same page in the classroom, then you enrich students who already have an understanding of the concept. We spend way too much time on intervention and not enough time on enrichment, causing students who should be advanced to move backward in student performance.

Also, even when students are given an intervention to understand, you still have to gravitate them back to the traditional format. Students have to know that intervention is a temporary solution to assist the learning. I say this because students cannot pull out manipulatives during a summative exam (e.g., state assessment, benchmark, ACT, SAT and so on).

Jet I-Mind Trick

This is a game of chess against checkers, and the students are playing chess. By this, I mean that students are using their street wit to get their way during class time. For example, students text each other when they want to meet in the hallway. They also place an earplug in their ear to prove they are not listening to their music or wear hoods to hide headphones and claim they have a headache, or lastly, use online teachers edition textbook to solve workbook problems, and the list goes on.

Stay away from students attempting to befriend you so now you are friends on social media and communicate outside of school and school activities. Teachers are supposed to present themselves in a light where students can learn how to be productive when entering the workforce, college, or trade. Allow students to grow for the time they are with you and move on. This is why you do not have time to form relationships with students. There are thousands more waiting for you the following year. The sooner you can promote or graduate a student, the better you can provide a positive service to someone else possibly in need of the same service or more.

Kagan Strategies

The reason Kagan Strategies Structures play an important role in learning because it provides everyone with a responsibility while in a group setting. The problem with group work is that students who are doing the work are being taken advantage of because they have to do their work as well as others in the group.

If purposeful, this is a great team learning activity because it gives students a chance to learn from one another and understand roles and responsibilities. This could assist them as they enter the workforce.

Lesson Plans

The purpose of lesson plans is to help the teacher develop a method for transferring the knowledge they have to the student. If teachers spend more time on the plan than instructing, the plan is a waste of time. Some schools have compliance issues and have to include a lot of wasted material in their plan, but as the teacher, you have to determine what items are necessary for discussion and what items just stay written.

If you spend two hours planning for a sixty-minute class, then your plan is not purposeful. When students are failing, the teacher should be able to complete everything in their plan because it is pertinent to what the students need to know.

Lesson plans should not cause so much frustration. If I have to write lesson plans for each day then my plan should only include material for that day.

As an administrator, when reviewing lesson plans, I should be able to determine what the student will learn and how they are going to apply what they learned. It does not need to include page numbers, textbooks, and types of material being used. Administrators can see this when they observe the teacher.

Administrators, please learn to remove some of the items from the teacher's plate so they can be more effective. Wherever I was an administrator, I would always attempt to remove something off the teacher's plate. We cannot continue to pile on responsibilities for the teacher and expect 100 percent effectiveness. We are already blaming teachers for students failing, but if we are a school with a positive culture, it is not just the teachers who need to make adjustments. We have to be considerate in understanding the teacher's role and what we ask of them.

I think administrators, at times, have been out of the classroom for so long that they have forgotten what it is like to manage 120 or more students. Now, if you take that into consideration and add it with the following, I think teachers have a case. Educators have to write lesson plans, make phone calls home, complete grades / progress reports / report cards, grade papers, attend meetings, write or implement information for IEPs, write or implement information for ELL strategies, create homework (hopefully), create class assignments, give assessments / review data with students, deliver instruction while covering multiple learning styles in order to reach *all* students, discipline students, take field trips, coach extracurricular activities, take attendance, morning duty / afternoon duty, monitor lunch/recess, and meet with parents/administrators/coaches.

I hope I made a point here, and I know these are things that come with the job; however, as an administrator, if you can remove some things off the teacher's plate, I guarantee you it will increase teacher's morale and performance.

I can go on with teacher responsibilities, but I think you understand. I am trying to say that, maybe the workload contributes to the lack of effectiveness due to exhaustion.

Lastly, I hear this comment all the time from educators, and I just want to provide my opinion. Anyone should not be able to come into a classroom and perform what's in a lesson plan. Teaching is an art, not a task. If anyone could do it, going to college would have served no purpose. I think we have to be more respectful in how we speak of education if we intend to reestablish a good education value.

Below is a lesson plan that I have used with my staff members, and they greatly appreciate how it is decreased to only focus on the day and closes with an assessment. Using this plan has allowed me to turn four schools around academically that were in a failing status.

Name:	Date:
Standard:	Subject:
I Do: How will you model your expectation?	For this section of the plan, the teacher models the expectation of the students. He/she must mandate that students adhere to modeling. During this time, students should not be taking notes or working ahead. This is time for them to watch and get a visual of the expectation.
Check for understanding. How will you address the class to see how many students had an understanding of what you modeled?	This is where you would use a formative assessment to determine how well the standard was delivered.
We Do: How will you ensure students have a clear understanding of the expectation before sending them to complete their independent practice?	For this section of the plan, the teacher will review the modeled example and provide students with at least two additional examples of the same concept.

Check for understanding. How will you address the class to see how many students had an understanding of what you modeled?	This is where you would use a formative assessment to determine how well the instruction was delivered. Determine students who continue to struggle and create a small group with them. You should not send this group of students to complete the independent activity because you know they are not ready. Sending them to complete the activity unprepared is setting them up for failure.
You Do: Independent Activity	The teacher calls the students who still have not learned the concept to the small group area where you may have to differentiate the instruction to assist struggling students.
Assessment to determine knowledge retained:	

Lesson plan template.

Learning about Your Student

In order for you to have a clear understanding of poverty, you have to learn what it all entails. The best way to learn about poverty is to talk to those who have experienced it or are currently experiencing it. Many teachers fail in this category because they believe this is something they already know how to deal with, but the consistent referrals state differently.

If your students are impoverished, it would be a good idea to have some type of breakfast snack waiting for them. Usually, lack of proper nourishment is a major cause to students sleeping in class or being irritable in the morning. There are multiple ways to assist the students who need to ensure they have a fair start of the day as a school breakfast or snacks in the classroom such as bananas, apples, oranges, or cereal bars.

When students are impoverished, the following behaviors could occur:

a) The student is moody first thing in the morning.
b) The student is very aggressive when being spoken to and appears to be looking for a confrontation.
c) The student tends to sleep in the classroom.
d) The student has a lack of focus during instruction.
e) The student is consistently disruptive.

Having an awareness of such information about your students will be useful as you work on developing a rapport with them to improve their performance in class.

Mandate

Today, students must be mandated to participate. Students should not be allowed to sit in class for the entire lesson and not take part in the classroom activity when you are checking for understanding from each student. This rule should be established at the beginning of the year when creating a positive culture and discussing with students how the class will be focusing on the learning.

Avoid having to elicit for participation by creating an environment in which students want to learn and demonstrate their growth on a daily basis.

Mind over Matter

As an educator in the inner city, it will be extremely beneficial to you as the teacher when you can convince students they can achieve what they believe to be the impossible: becoming an A student. Achieving this is done by establishing trust and support when needed.

Students have to believe and see evidence that what you are saying is true. When I worked at an alternative high school, students did not believe they would graduate from high school because of how far behind they were. I had a student attending the school with half a credit, and in 2020, he proudly announced that he was graduating.

I remember sometime in 2019 when I crossed a Will Smith YouTube video in which he discussed the importance of believing you can and setting your mind to believing you can to overcome matter. I thought this was one of the most powerful videos I have ever seen because it was short, sweet and direct.

However, the most important piece to the puzzle is making sure you believe in what you are saying as well. It is one thing to discuss what you want to occur and it's another to ensure that it happens. Older students in school are led by action and not by word of mouth.

Therefore, daily, I would demonstrate the change that was needed, why it was needed, and how it was going to benefit us at the estimated deadline. Time was short, so I had to move quickly in executing my plan. Here are a few of the steps I took, as an administrator, to help students get on board with the plan:

1. Assemble the appropriate team that could help me accomplish the goal.
2. Hold morning assemblies by weekly to continually review the plan with the students.
3. Hold weekly staff meetings to address any concerns I had with staff making progress
4. Identify the end goal and how we were going to get there.
5. Use posters to remind students of the plan (e.g., no cursing in school, student growth displayed with increasing attendance rates while decreasing referrals, and suspensions).
6. Reward students for minor accomplishments.
7. When possible, communicate the plan with stakeholders.
8. Develop partnerships that could share in showing students *we care.*

9. Support students with change as we know this could be difficult for anyone.
10. Be there for students to lift them in lieu of kicking them while they are down.

In one year and a half, here are things we were able to accomplish: *all* seniors graduated in 2018, job opportunities were provided to *all* seniors through my Home Depot partnership, eight full-ride scholarships were offered for students to attend Paradise Valley Community College, ten thousand dollars were given to our school in donation money, and lastly, according to state exams, we were labeled as a B school and the district received that status for the first time since opening twenty years prior.

What I learned from all this is that you can achieve whatever you believe. I am so proud of my students as they enter the workforce with a better chance of surviving due to accomplishing what they believed was unachievable—graduating from high school.

Needs Assessment

Needs assessment pertains to a survey of stakeholders' responses to get feedback on what they believe the school needs from their perspective. Often, I see schools attempting to complete this process once a year.

The reason you are not seeing growth is that you are not allotting the time needed to see growth. A needs assessment should be completed every three years where you can collect enough data to determine what programs truly are effective or not. Once that data has been collected and analyzed, you can monitor and adjust.

Overt Learning

Teachers, please make sure to have students recall information they have read when giving silent reading time. Unfortunately, many students do not enjoy pleasure reading during the school day, so when assigning this type of activity, be sure to make it purposeful.

Overt activities can assist students in increasing their writing skills. Writing is a subject that should be taken more seriously in the field of education, especially if we are following college and career readiness standards.

For anyone who has gone to college, you know the importance of writing, as it was applied to every subject that I had. Students should be writing as much as they are reading. Increasing one subject without the other will only get you 50 percent.

As a result of students not writing, they have difficulty expressing themselves appropriately in written format. When this occurs, students become frustrated and refuse to respond or will address the question incorrectly just to be done with the question.

To avoid this from occurring in the classroom, have students start completing small writing assignments Begin with having students write sentences before attempting to make them write paragraphs. When building confidence in a student regarding their academics, you want to focus on small data that is being chunked, then build from there. This will allow you to monitor and adjust as needed while continuing the learning for other students.

Positive Communication

Teachers, this strategy will help you win the battle of getting the parents on your side. As educators, we report data more than anything else associated with our profession. We report to parents, principals, boards, state department, federal department, agencies, students, each other, stakeholders, donators, media, and anything else that relates to student performance.

Therefore, it is important that you practice the use of positive communication. For example, just because you are underperforming does not mean you need to bash the school, its programs, or leaders unless it is greatly justified.

When communicating with parents, consider the number of hostile phone calls they may receive about their child. Eventually, a negative is created between the school and the parent regardless of fault.

If you can find a way to call the worse behaved student in your class and possibly the school and leave a positive comment with the parents about something the student did to improve their academics monthly, you will win that parent and student over for the remainder of the year.

Once trust has been established, the teacher should begin to connect with the student to track their data to show the instant student growth. You want to focus on this strategy for at least the entire quarter, making adjustments as needed.

Data conversations with the student about their progress should be positive and monthly. This time will also help in building a rapport with your student, so use it wisely.

Proactive Leaders

This strategy is important, as it pertains to preparation and planning. Teachers who are still gathering copies in the morning to prepare for the day are reactive, not proactive. Working smarter not harder is often stated but rarely followed.

Teachers, if you can, lessen your planning and only focus on what you can complete in that time frame with some form of assessment to review data, you will begin to see improvement made in your planning, preparation, delivery, and outcome.

This strategy helps when planning for differentiated instruction. When you are not prepared for the day, teachers default to direct instruction, causing subgroup students in need of assistance for following along to fall behind in the learning.

Quality/Quantity

Teachers, please make sure students present quality work over the amount of work they are expected to complete. When students are aware that quality matters, they will begin to put more effort into their work.

Students like to showcase their ability, but they are still considered children or teenagers, meaning they will do less if given the opportunity. Remember that everyone is not going to college; therefore, students who are not considered to be as intellectual as maybe someone going to college don't necessarily see the benefit of perfection or striving for it.

This thought process can easily be overcome by establishing this rule at the beginning of the student's entrance into your classroom. When students are aware of the expectation for *all* assignments given, they will work hard to reach the level of acceptance.

When you diminish your requirements for the quality of work you expect for that assignment, you are saying to the students they can do less and still meet the teacher's expectation.

I remember debating this belief with a special education teacher about an assignment she decided to display. The assignment was for younger grade levels, and I believe it had to do with vocabulary words and coloring. The words that were displayed were misspelled, and the crayons used were outside the picture lines.

When I asked the teacher why she was displaying this work, she told me that it was okay because the student was in the special education program and that he/she did her best in completing the assignment. I immediately responded by asking the teacher, "If the student wanted to, could they have done a better job and completed the work with a little more assistance?" And the teacher responded yes.

Here is my concern as an administrator. Why would any teacher accept an incomplete assignment from a student when you know they could do better? As educators, our goal should be to push students to do their very best in all assignments, and when they still fall below our expectation, we—as educators, guides, and mentors—should show them how to achieve more.

By following this practice, you will get the student to review their work before turning it in for completion to ensure the quality is sufficient for a passing grade. When students do not check their work, quality is not a priority.

Here is another tip you can use if you agree that this is a teacher's concern. Get in the habit of evaluating a student's work using a rubric. By doing this, you can set the tone for students meeting your expectations.

I would only start off with two columns in the rubric. This will remove the grey areas of scoring by having pass/fail with details as your score. Once students do not meet the requirement for passing, do not tell them why they did not meet the requirement. Have the student refer back to the rubric and identify what they missed in order to get a passing score. If they can find their mistake and show you where they went wrong, then that should represent the quality of effort. Now have them redo that assignment and reward them with a flattering compliment if not an announcement of how proud you are of them for their diligence in wanting to display quality.

When you are focused on quantity, the amount of work given to a student to demonstrate their level of understanding becomes too overwhelming, and you can cause the student to shut down. For example, it does not take fifty math problems to determine if the student understands the concept. You are also providing more work for yourself since you have to grade the assignment. This takes us back to the theory of working smarter, not harder. To increase your longevity in this profession, make sure work provided is purposeful.

The Three Rs

At some point, students have to go back to the basics if they continue to be unsuccessful in the classroom. If there is no outlining reason explaining the student's low academic performance, then the student is probably missing so many foundational skills. You have to go back to the basics for them to move forward.

Many leaders feel you can bypass this step, and this is why so many students continue to suffer. Lack of knowledge in any academic skill impacts all subjects negatively. As discussed earlier in the passage, reading and writing must go hand and hand. Arithmetic is of equal value and should hold the same merit as the other two subjects.

If you allot time in your learning to always review the basics when working with small groups, you will begin to see growth in those areas. This will also serve as a great strategy for assisting ELL students in the classroom.

State of Academic Emergency

I am not sure if this is something real or not, but if it is, I would definitely like to know how to go about calling this for our country and any states that are suffering, to make academic growth in comparison to other countries and states.

With the dropout rate numbers increasing in the state of Arizona and the number of students attending school underperforming in the state, it seems as though this is something we should consider a priority.

If we have been underperforming as a state for decades, I am afraid to say that academics is not a priority for our students. Here is an example of why I say this. When you have one of the highest teacher shortages in the country and you do not make the necessary changes to prevent this from continuing, such as increasing the states average daily membership (ADM) to attract more teachers to the area, then we are saying to our children that education is important but not a priority.

Standards

When students are dropping out of school at a tremendous rate, and students in school are not performing academically upon completing graduation requirements, we find more students getting jobs as opposed to careers, and we know the majority of students are not going to college, I am going to take the risk and say that maybe college and career readiness standards are not the proper guidelines for what we are attempting to accomplish with our youth.

Teachers, we teach students standards for them to be successful when displaying the learning acquired for that lesson, term, and year. When you do not have a check and balance system such as a state assessment and students are underperforming, I do not understand the sense of urgency in attempting to cover all standards prior to the year end.

As a teacher, you can reach higher levels of your instruction if you slow your pace down and spend more time in depth with what you are teaching. Give students a better understanding of the concept being taught by taking the lesson through higher Bloom's taxonomy levels and forcing students to use critical thinking skills while exploiting their creativity.

Teaching

I believe the problem with teaching is its multiple meanings. Everyone seems to have a different belief of what teaching actually means. I hope that I am able to relate to many of you by the meaning I provide as an administrator.

Teaching involves planning a lesson that one can deliver to one's class and ensure that the information was transferred to its recipients. Assessments will be used to determine the effectiveness of the lesson's delivery. Based on the data submitted, the teacher will determine if enrichment, intervention, or reteaching is necessary. Students should meet the academic bar of 75 percent or higher in each activity before moving on the next lesson or standard taught.

If students cannot prove they are learning, how do you prove that you are teaching?

Understanding Poverty

You can't teach what you don't know. Poverty is a serious situation that seems to be growing within our youth. If educating students in poverty, please be sure to be patient, forgiving, and understanding when a student appears to be disruptive because he/she is probably disruptive due to hunger.

A quick fix to assisting students with this concern is to have snacks somewhere in the room where students can put something into their stomachs. I know that many schools have a rule about making sure students do not eat in the classroom, but if the only thing stopping you and the student from connecting is where to eat, then please have another area, maybe just outside the classroom, where they can have a snack before starting their day.

By observing your students throughout the day and asking your coworkers about their behavior during team meetings, you should be able to identify a few clues without asking any questions. I say reframe from questions due to cultural differences and not knowing what you should be asking.

For example, I remember a teacher asking a student about being so tired during class. The teacher decided to hold the student back after class to discuss why he was so tired. Being young and naive, the student did not think anything of it, so he began to inform the teacher that he had to share food with his siblings and they kept him up all night tossing and turning. Next, the teacher began to ask why he and his siblings were sharing a bed. Again, not knowing, the student began to discuss his discomfort with the situation. And here it comes. The teacher informed the student that this was unfair to his education and that it was interrupting his learning.

Well, when the student got home, his parents asked him how his day was, and as usual, the student began to discuss the conversation he had with his teacher, and his father was irate. He immediately called the school in such a rage and then said he was on his way to the school to meet with the teacher. This was a major concern because he definitely did not plan to have a peaceful conversation with the teacher.

Luckily, I was at the school and was able to intervene because I knew the parent. After meeting with the parent, I was able to calm the parent down and ensure that no one was attempting to cause harm or pry into any family concerns. The teacher was just trying to see if she could help.

The reason I related this problem to cultural differences is that although the teacher assumed she was asking legitimate questions to the student, she never considered the parent and what he/she might think about their child being interrogated.

If the family is experiencing stressful times due to poverty, and finds out that their child is being questioned without their permission, then as far as the parent is concerned, the teacher is attempting to say that he is not raising his child appropriately and that assistance is needed.

Here is something that I would always tell my teachers, as an administrator, about questioning students or parents. Remember, it is not about what you say or how you say it rather than how it is perceived. The teacher could have asked her questions as pleasantly as possible, but to that parent, the teacher is not the one who should be asking those types of questions.

Lastly, I recall when a student had just arrived to school and was extremely late. The teacher was new to the school and did not know the student yet. When the student went to class, the teacher read the student the riot act for being late.

Before you know it, the student exploded by yelling and screaming at the teacher. She had enough and refused to listen to anything else the teacher had to say. As the teacher began to raise her voice, it now became a yelling match between the teacher and student. When I arrived, the two had been separated from each other to prevent any further trouble from occurring. After the situation had calmed down and I met with the student to see what happened, the parent called. I had just found out that the family has been evicted, but wanted to still come to school.

The parent said they advised the student not to come due to her hostility over what happened but could not stop the student. The student was a senior in school and knew she needed to be in school if she wanted to graduate on time.

The moral to this story is this: if you are concerned about a student and only that student, then you should never address your concern with that student in front of other students. More than anything else, student was embarrassed about others finding out why she was late, and what impact would that have on her reputation in school from this point on?

As a teacher, try your best to know your students. You should be able to identify which students participate the most, who may need further assistance, who gets distracted easily, and who you can count on always to give 100 percent. You can determine all this without having a relationship with students but simply by just focusing on the learning. By focusing on the learning, the rest will come to light.

By having this information, it becomes easier to be more proactive with planning and executing your delivery.

Uniformity

Nothing displays uniformity more than seeing a school, its students, teachers, and administration all in the same harmony with one another. This is when you really get to see the benefits of your hard work. Some of my best compliments from parents were how happy they were to be on campus helping throughout the day.

Having young students (K–8) transition in an orderly manner will always make your school appear to be welcoming and safe for parents to leave their children with you.

Vocational Education

It is so disheartening to see how this particular form of education seems to have left the school system. I am not sure if such programs were removed due to testing or safety expenses, but I believe this skill will always be needed.

Students should be encouraged to either go to college or learn a trade. Sometimes, educators, drive students away from school because we are always trying to steer them toward college, when all they would like to do is continue their family legacy, a trade (e.g., plumbing, mechanics, construction, demolition, and the list goes on).

If not for education, my lifelong dream would be to build my own house. When my cousin, Gerard, got married in California, I was exposed to what I always thought I wanted to do. Gerard had a sister whose husband was in construction, and he was building his own home. I was so impressed because he was doing it himself and even installing an elevator. When I had the chance to speak with him about what inspired him to build his own home, he said he got his idea and inspiration from school.

Today, many schools have vocational learning programs but it is through the computer. This practice will never compete with the experience you receive from hands-on learning.

My tip for teachers pertaining to this topic is, whenever possible, please take full advantage of tactile learning. You never know what you may inspire your students to do.

With-it-ness

This is one of those phrases like "and whatnot" that has no place in the English language, but everyone seems to know its intent. What I like most about this phrase is how every time I heard the phrase by the curriculum specialist in Roosevelt School District No. 66, she displayed the meaning simultaneously.

The phrase refers to how one diversifies himself/herself during an allotted time frame. You can associate it to differentiation. We often used it as we prepared for gallery walks.

When applying differentiated strategies during your instruction, the teacher's most important thing to remember is keeping an eye on the whole group while working with smaller groups. Teachers get so wrapped up in working with struggling students that they tend to forget the majority, which later leads to classroom disruptions.

When the teacher applies this to their instruction, he/she is in full operating mode. This is not an easy task to apply; however, if you can master this strategy, you will be considered an authoritative leader where everyone benefits and no child is left behind (literally).

This teacher is able to assist small groups, answer questions, use the chalkboard, refer to terms, and assess students throughout the hour. Students are engaged in the activity and ask questions to challenge their learning. The classroom is a warm environment conducive to teaching and learning. In an ideal setting, this is how *all* teachers should instruct.

(X—Not applicable to this reading)

Year after Year after Year

This is when the same outcome continues to occur—a failing status. It is very difficult to maintain a positive morale during this time when you feel as though nothing is ever going change. When schools fail continuously, you cannot blame the teachers and leave out everyone else who contributes to such redundancy.

Leaders play a major role in students underperforming, and when I say leaders, I am speaking from the top down. Once you begin to separate the team, the dominos will fall and blame will begin to take over. Unfortunately, many leaders at the top (superintendent/CEO) will never see themselves as a part of the problem when the school is failing, and that is the problem.

When you place someone who does not have a background in education in charge of a learning institution and things go wrong, do not look far. You are only as good as your leader.

Airport Zip Code Project

This was an amazing event put on by leaders across the 85034 zip code. Together, the leaders were able to assemble over 60 vendors for giving back to the community. Students received job opportunities, haircuts, clothing, gifts, prizes, and much more. A video of this amazing display of caring and giving can be found on YouTube at Airport Zip Code Project (Career Success).

Principal's Message

To my peers, I hope you found some items mentioned here that you could implement into your schools or classrooms ASAP. Please know that I intend to help and not hinder you. In order to make a change, rocks have to be overturned.

I know you are working very hard, and I wish you all the best in having a great 2020 academic year. Maybe this pandemic will bring some light to the classroom, school, and learning. No matter what, please ensure that students are being educated and not monitored.

I have attached a few strategies that have worked wonders for me as an administrator and director of education. Hopefully, you can find positive use for the material as well.

Parent-Teacher Conference

Please change when you have parent-teacher conferences to make it more beneficial for parents who already struggle in attending. Many inner-city parents work multiple jobs or long hours and possibly miss time off work to show you and their child how much they care about the child's education.

Unfortunately, when they miss time from work, it is not usually paid time off. I can't think of anything more upsetting, as an administrator, than having a parent rush to a conference, and the teacher says, "Sorry but there is nothing we can do at this point because the term is over, but maybe next term we can address the concern."

Why does a parent need to miss out on money for that information? Isn't that something you could have e-mailed or called the parent to express?

To assist my parents, I moved parent teacher conference closer to midterm progress reports, giving the parent at least four to five weeks to make adjustments with their child if needed. Following the conference, I had teachers send two progress reports home prior to the term ending. Now no one can say they were not informed that their child was failing.

Also, if you have not moved to this style of conferences yet, please do so. It will make things so much easier on the teachers.

Students should be facilitating conferences with their parents, with you as the teacher in the background waiting to answer questions. Have the student explain why they did not complete their work, study for the assessment, or were absent from class since last week.

The sooner you begin to hold the student accountable for their actions, the sooner you will start to see the student's change.

*****

Please create an effective management plan and rid your school of discipline. Discipline is a form of punishment. How can you discipline students but not be in favor of corporal punishment?

Students should only endure consequences for their actions and should be held responsible for those consequences. Our job as educators is to educate, not parent. Too many teachers get wrapped up into parenting instead of teaching. We have one job, do it well. This is what we are paid to do. The rest is fluff.

Students get scholarships for being well educated. Students go into career paths for having a solid education in a particular career choice, and jobs are provided to students for knowing a trade. Basically, the student says, "Please just educate me, I can take care of the rest!"

Yes, our job does entail much responsibility, but the payoff is well worth it. Having a student say thank you, in the end, makes it all worthwhile.

It's amazing to see how many leaders are not able to stop violence in schools. Violence in schools today is not as we once knew it to be. Prohibiting violence should be a daily activity if it is something you are having difficulty controlling.

*****

Please reinstate field trips. This activity is extremely beneficial for English Language learners. If students only speak Spanish in their home and the state removed the four-hour block, this is the only time outside of school when students get a chance to adhere the English language.

Students have more appreciation for school when they are a part of something fun. However, the trip should not favor the teachers more than the student. Sometimes the teacher chooses the trip based on his/her wants and not based on what the student wants.

If you are in the process of turning a school around, it is important that you have certified employees who have acquired the necessary strategies needed for working with slower developing students.

Students Teaching Students

This should be unacceptable. Teachers like to use the excuse students learn better from other students at times, instead of the teacher.

Students should not learn better from other students. The student just explains it better than you. If the student can do your job, why does the school have you?

Teachers, your job requires an art and skill in performing it. Neither students nor noneducators should be able to perform your job better than you. If they can, that is a problem. You did not go college for someone to do your job better than you without the four years of schooling that you have acquired.

Students go to school to learn, not to teach. How do parents feel about their child's academic time being spent helping struggling students instead of being enriched in their own learning? Unfortunately, this is never a one-time event, which is why I am bringing it up as a concern. If you focus on enriching the helpers, it could inspire the others.

Things That You Make You Go Hmmm

In the state of Arizona when schools fall in the bottom 25 percent of the state's average academically, they have the potential of being awarded additional millions to improve their academics. If this grant is approved for your district, the district will receive additional monies for three years, and if the school has not improved within those three years, they could reapply for the grant for another three years.

Do not get me wrong. I believe the state should provide assistance to underperforming schools, but not to the point where teachers enjoy failure due to the additional funding received.

I researched various professions attempting to find what other professional organizations provide additional millions for failure. Professional sports teams pay teams additionally for winning the championship while corporations and stockholders give employees bonuses for overachieving. Maybe, and it's just a thought, but maybe if we gave schools additional funding for doing well, it will inspire other schools to work a little harder.

In Arizona, the state eliminated the state assessment, and now there is nothing that holds students accountable for their learning and, more so, graduating. Unfortunately, many students failed the assessment yearly, but removing it did not improve schools' academic performance.

At the very least, by having a state assessment, you knew that when students graduated from high school, they acquired a set of skills that will allow them to perform basic tasks required by many occupations.

In the state of Arizona, there is a law that allows students to miss up to ten consecutive days before the state removes the student from the school's roster. Students exploit this law in the inner city by missing multiple days of the quarter but never reaching ten consecutively, so the days start over. Students must understand that cannot pass the class by not attending class, yet they still do.

Since we do not have an assessment to hold students accountable for learning, maybe we can institute a law stating that students have to attend school a certain number of days as a requirement for graduating.

Academically Challenged Leaders (ACL)

This is a term that refers only to people in powerful administrative positions but cannot make effective administrative decisions due to a lack of education. When you place someone in a leadership position such as a superintendent's, CEO's, or principal's and cannot make a difference in the school, start to rebuild from there.

Examples of ACL Decisions That Drastically Affect Student Learning

The CEO decides to refinance the school's land so they can purchase additional property for the school. When asked what is going to be built on the additional land, the CEO said he/she is not sure because they did not refinance for enough money to build something. It is only enough money to purchase the land. Then they say, "Maybe we can sell hot dogs and hamburgers to build on the property." (Are you kidding me?)

The superintendent purchases an enriched curriculum used to prep students for college at an underperforming school that has students who are multiple grade levels behind. As it turns out, the reading content is too difficult for the students, the teaching content is too challenging for the teachers, and as you know it, the students suffer. (Are you kidding me?)

How many red flags, in education, is enough for someone to make change?

Below is my affirmation with working under an academically challenged leader.

As mentioned earlier in the text, 2018–2019 was an extremely productive year for me, and I was in a historical battle with my friend and coworker for becoming superintendent for the following year, 2019–2020. The charter holder announced through emails to the district for six months that she wanted someone internal for the position.

Although all principals of the four schools were invited to apply, Kelly Shieck was my concern, who happens to be from Michigan. The old rivalry even made it inside the classroom. Kelly is a phenomenal principal, and I knew it would not be easy winning this game.

The battle was on, and we went hard to prove our qualifications and to balance the playing field academically for inner-city students. We were off to a great start. We both achieved accolades that shined in our school. During this time, the marketing director was working with both principals to promote some of the new programs our schools were bringing to the table.

When we had administrative meetings, Kelly and I would often refer to the Ohio State-Michigan rivalry for fun, but either one of us would have supported the other one unconditionally.

Prior to the grand announcement toward the end of the year of who will become superintendent, we were told that that marketing director convinced the charter holder that we needed a curriculum audit to determine why the schools have been performing so poorly in previous years.

Remember, this was my first full academic year at this time so I was still figuring things out and trying to see how a marketing director advises someone on academics. Since he was a former superintendent, the charter holder agreed to the audit, and the new auditor happened to be his wife. Go figure.

Although this would have been a red flag for me (because at the time we did not even have a curriculum, so how do you audit what we do not have?), I had to remain focused. Nevertheless, my mind was on the superintendent position, so I did not pay too much attention to the powerful chess move being made.

The time had arrived, and we gathered at the elementary school to hear the announcement. The charter holder said was she was told none of the candidates were ready for such a position, and therefore, the position was given to the auditor. First red flag. Minus five yards.

Even though we were angered at how this all went down, we were given a large increase to ease the pain, so it wasn't as bad as it sounded, and we knew the work needed to redirect the district, so we all accepted the fact and moved on.

The year had ended, and it was time to go to work. We hit the ground running with the most non purposeful meetings ever. It was then that we, as principals, knew this was going to be a hectic year because the new leader wanted to change everything. Although much change was needed, veteran principals knew change was difficult and should be taken gradually.

Throughout the summer and especially at the beginning of the year, the schools received endless emails about our new leaders and how they have been banned from Tucson due to unethical practice, non-professionalism, and a host of other items mentioned in Google. There were at least three emails per week for months about not allowing our new leaders to destroy our students' learning. The emails were anonymous, so the charter holder ignored them and advised the employees to do the same.

However, the emails appeared to have reached the charter board and the state board, so at the end of 2018, one of the boards decided to pay a visit to one of the schools, and it was the school where the marketing director had taken over as principal for the last few months. I was unsure what the board members reviewed by not being present but was told they looked at files and asked questions.

To no avail, we went into the new year, and it was exhausting. Red flag after red flag. It seemed as though we were on a moving vehicle with no breaks and no destination in mind. I had never felt so lost in something I took great pride in knowing, education.

Second flag. Minus five yards. Day one of the school year started, and we were told that our daily hours were incorrect and how the new leader could not believe how this could happen. We informed the sup that we have used the same hours since school had opened over twenty years ago, and the state had approved them yearly, so how was this possible?

After hiring two consultants on this so-called problem, we worked on changing our schedule and hours for months and still never got it right (if there was anything to get right).

Next, we decided to purchase a curriculum. We rushed through three curriculum presentations in three days, only to purchase the worse curriculum ever for the students we served. The curriculum presenter asked the sup during his presentation, "Are you sure you want to use this curriculum? It is designed for enriched learning? Why?"

By having a blocked schedule and half a year representing a whole year, the presenter knew this curriculum would not be a good choice for us, but the sup wanted it so. She asked if the presenter could create a pacing guide for block scheduling. Third red flag. Minus five yards. If a presenter attempts to warn you about utilizing something his team developed, you should probably adhere to the warning.

Since the school year had started and normally curriculum orders are made a half a year or so in advance, we had to wait months for the curriculum to arrive. When it did, it was without the required readings needed for certain topics so now that had to be ordered as well.

While waiting on the curriculum, the sup wanted to begin work-ing on some improvement plan, and we informed her that we already have ALEAT, and it is a work-in-progress program required by the Arizona Department of Education (ADE). Since she was unaware of

ALEAT, we had to create an equivalent document to ALEAT. Fourth red flag, minus five yards. I believe in working smarter, not harder.

By the fourth week of school, the sup wanted us to utilize some new tracking system for grades that demonstrated growth or lack of it. Please make no mistake about it. Data is crucial in turning a school around, but what data would we track without the curriculum?

Now, we were on our third consultant, and he was working with us on utilizing this SIMS data tracking system and assessment tool. The presentation did not go well because the presenter was not informed of what we wanted out of using the system. So there were another eight hours of wasted time. Teachers felt overwhelmed already, and we were just in the first quarter of the school year.

Eventually, the curriculum arrived, and delivering it was complete chaos. Regardless of what we said we needed based on enrollment, we could not get the numbers right. Each school had to beg and borrow textbooks, and as new students arrived, we had to order more.

Now that we had a new curriculum, we hired two new consultants who were using the curriculum at their school for enriched classes. Guess what the new consultants for the math and reading curriculums said when they arrived at our school?

"Why are you guys using this curriculum?"

They, too, knew it was not designed for our purpose, and since they were being paid, they tried to make it work. Their goal was to design a pacing guide for teachers to follow. After observing teachers and attending administrative meetings for a few weeks, they eventually disappeared with no explanation from the sup of what happened. Fifth flag. Minus five yards.

Now, the sup decided to hire a language arts teacher and a second-year math teacher as specialists for developing the pacing guide and holding meetings with teachers to guide them effectively on following the guide, using the assessment tool, create weekly mini-quizzes, and track the data. (Are you kidding me? What the hell is going on around here?)

The principals informed the sup that this was not a good idea. The teachers had no experience in educational leadership because they were new to the profession. After making two attempts at their task, they realized the difficulty in what was being requested.

At our next administrative meeting, the sup wanted to discuss school data. We informed her then that we did not have the data to discuss because the specialist had not been creating assessments for students to take; therefore, there was no data to discuss. When one of the principals informed the sup that they should not still be receiving a stipend because they were not performing the task, the sup told the principal that it was not her concern and expected each school to present data at the next meeting.

(At this midpoint, I want you to know that you cannot make this —— up, and I am not done explaining the year.)

Now, the supplemental reading material had arrived. Teachers were expected to fully utilize all materials purchased as directed by our sup. Imagine trying to have students who struggle with reading, attempting to read *Beowulf, Schindler's List,* or any other enriched literature. It sounded like a DJ mixing and scratching on the turntables as students struggled to read a line in the text. Students who are forced to read above their level is surely a fast way to get students not to want to read again, and it's not because they do not like reading. It's because of the embarrassment you created in having them read material that is too challenging for them.

Out of the clear blue comes a Title 1 specialist who had our emails and was requesting that material be sent to her ASAP as it pertained to Title 1 and school improvement. A simple question was asked: "Who are you? Why do we have to submit this material all of a sudden?" Again, we were told that the sup hired her; this info was needed for title/school improvement funding. The specialist seemed to be a nice person, but 1, we were in suspense with who or what was next on the list.

Be careful what you ask for. Now we had a new consultant (sixth red flag, minus five yards), and her task was to guide administrators on how to complete an observation and evaluation for teachers. This was hilarious, seeing how I developed the observation tool that the district was using and had used it since I arrived.

Early in my administrative career, I went to the Arizona School Administrators (ASA) training on evaluations and accurately completed an evaluation. I even completed up to level 3, which was the more advanced level training.

This was one of the best trainings I had ever had. ASA is compiled of veteran superintendents and leaders who have made a difference in education. This training has led to my success as an administrator, and I am ecstatic to say I received it from ASA.

Sorry, I digressed. I brought this to your attention because, as administrators, we were treated as though we never completed an eval before. Three out of the four administrators have already been a principal for more than ten years.

We were told by this consultant that we had to complete two evaluations, and it was already after the Christmas break. Again, frustration was at its highest level for teachers and administrators. Teachers were irritated because of the constant change. What would happen to their jobs if they did not comply? Administrators were irritated because they could not be there for their teachers due to the additional responsibilities.

By now, teachers and administrators were so lost and confused, everyone went into confinement to avoid creating any further waves with the Supt.

Now, after the break, the principal of our main campus and I was told to attend a state-run data meeting along with our school state rep and sup. Kelly and I were informed we turned our schools around from an F to a B for the school year 2018–2019. This was the first time any school in the district had a passing score per state assessment, and neither the sup nor did the charter holder felt this was newsworthy enough to be told throughout the district.

Also, it was at this state meet when the sup told the state rep during lunch that she did not believe in diplomas. To her, they were just a piece of paper that meant nothing. She felt algebra was a waste of time teaching to students. Seventh red flag, minus ten yards.

I discussed this earlier in the book, and I will repeat it, do not assume that because you do not use something you learned during school for your professional career, then it speaks for everyone else. I am grateful for learning algebra and all other school subjects, which allows me to be versatile in life and my career choices.

As a former school improvement specialist, there was no way my cadre would not have done something about that comment and, at the very least, informed our supervisor of what was said to us. I immediately replied to the comment by saying, "I believe in both, and as principal, it is my goal to assist all students in receiving a high school diploma and help students learn algebra and beyond." When we returned from this meeting, Kelly and I could not believe what the sup said and wanted to ensure state rep knew we disagreed with that belief. I was not sure what the state rep did with that information, but it must have been dropped from what I saw.

Now that we were back at schools, Kelly and I had turned in our last application to hire an ELL coach. Hiring was removed from all principals, and we had to go through the sup in order for it to be approved (eighth red flag, minus 5 yards). This was a first for me in over thirteen years since I did not have the approval to hire as principal. It was embarrassing to tell an applicant that they had to go through another interview with the sup to be hired. Most of them said, "You don't make that decision as principal?"

This was so upsetting because we had over one hundred immigrants of whom many were preemergent, but the sup refused to provide them any service with learning the English language. These students moved around at the main campus as a cohort the entire day, with no assistance with the English language, and the sup's office was at this school. Did I mention the sup was a former ELL student herself, hmm?

The next new task was to implement the computers that were just purchased (ninth red flag, minus five yards). How do you go from paper and pencil in the middle of the year to computers for all assignments? This was an alternative school. We were still working on improving attendance, and she wanted us to do what!

On top of everything else, we had to determine how students would use the computers, how the computers would be dispersed, how to track the computers since students get out of school at different times, and how to hold students accountable for the computers.

By now, we were drained and just trying to get through the year. The district had become extremely toxic, and there was no trust. Teachers and administrators were being used against one another to keep the sup informed about gossip.

To help pick spirits up throughout the district, Dr. Fuginitti assembled a team that would pull off one of the most amazing events at a school. We were a part of the Airport Zip Code (85034) Project, and we had over 60 vendors attending the school to provide opportunities for the community. It was great. Students, parents, and community members were all invited to receive food, clothes, gifts, prizes, jobs, haircuts, motivational speeches, televisions, and much more.

As time went by, we began to worry where the other students from the district were because it was getting late. The sup decided not to let students from the other schools attend. She said there was a new law that prohibited students from using the school bus to transport kids from school to school. We just looked at her and said, "Are you serious?" She assumed she could tell us anything. Therefore, it was only for my students, and since we had a small enrollment, the event was not as big as it could have been. It was still a great event and can be viewed on YouTube at Airport Zip Code Project for Career Success High Schools.

By now, we were into the third quarter. I was asked to be a committee member to determine if a junior high robotic program should be purchased for the high schools. This was a program that the marketing director that would be a great idea.

While taking notes during the presentation, the sup asked me if I had any questions before we closed, and I said, "As a matter of fact, I do." I asked the presenter to please show me some data on how this program improved the learning of at-risk students as mentioned in the presentation, and the presenter replied, "I do not have that information right now, but we'll get back to you." I said, "Okay, thank you." My next question was how the program assists special education students with their learning, and the presenter replied, "Sorry, I do not have that information, but I will get back to you."

So I asked, "How do you expect us to purchase a million-dollar robotic program for a junior high school and we are a high school, and you do not have any data to present on how it improves education for all?"

Well, the marketing director was pissed. You could see the steam coming off his face as if to say, "Who in the hell invited him to attend?"

Three weeks later, the sup was looking for directors for the following year and asked me to interview for the position. I knew I would not get the job but informed my staff I would try because they did not want to see us broken up. Teachers and staff told me it was the first time they ever worked in the district without being cursed out by students and seeing daily fights occur, and seeing students actually working to graduate. That is what I brought to them by focusing on the learning.

When I arrived for the interview, guess who was on the panel? It was the sup, her right-hand consultant, and the CEO of the robotic program who was not an educator, did not work for the school and had no interest in the school other than being the first AZ school to use his program.

At the end of the interview, the sup said, "Well, you may know everything there is to know, about education, but that still does not make you a good fit for the school."

I replied by saying, "Okay. Thank you for your time."

Three weeks later, I received an e-mail to meet the sup at my school. I asked what data I should ready but I got no response. When the sup arrived with a consultant (tenth red flag, minus ten yards), I was told that I did not get the job in which I interviewed for and my services were no longer needed. This was at the end of the third marking period after spring break, so it was late March. Covid-19 had just impaired the school system, and I was let go right at the end of the third marking period. I was told HR would give me my paperwork. To this day, August 2020, I do not know why I was released. I do not have my paperwork, causing me to file unemployment or obtain employment elsewhere because they would not provide me with evaluations or recommendations.

Kelly, the other principal, was also released after me. The most confusing thing is, why would they release me but pay me till the end of the school year? Although I am appreciative of it, it is not fair for them to release me but have my parents assume I am still there because they will not send a letter out informing parents I will not be scheduling classes for the fourth quarter.

When the quarter began, parents called my cell as it was connected to the school line (since we were working remotely), out of concern for their child graduating. I had to inform the parents that I was no longer an employee, so I could not help them.

This had to be the first time in education when two principals, who were the first in over twenty years to turn an F school to a B school, according to state assessments, were released before the year-end.

Additional Events That Led to a Frustrating Year Full of Red Flags

— The students are too mistreated, and they are none the wiser. They are not receiving the proper services for special education or English language learning. There are over one hundred students in the special education program in this district, and there is only one certified special education teacher and an uncertified special education assistant. Eleventh red flag, minus 10 yards.

— When substitutes are needed in this district, they use the special education teacher and cancel special education services for that day. (Guess how often that occurs). Twelfth red flag, minus 10 yards.

— Students in this district walked across the stage in 2018, only to attend school the following year for six more months because they did not have enough credits to walk. (Are you kidding me?) Thirteenth red flag, minus 15 yards.

— A student at this school in 2018 received a $500 award for graduating, only to be in school the following year up to Christmas break when he completed all credit requirements. Fourteenth red flag, minus 5 yards.

- Students attended school for seven hours a day with no electives, and they are in a block schedule, 90-minute classes with no materials other than the textbook and computers they haven't used thus far. The sup says there are not enough students to provide an elective teacher. Fifteenth red flag, minus 5 yards.
- Students at this school are allowed to retake classes they have already passed. Sixteenth red flag, minus 5 yards.
- Students in this district are given A letter grades for not coming to school. Some troubled students get higher grades than those who attend daily: Seventeenth red flag, minus 5 yards.
- In this district, seven consultants, were working to improve instruction throughout the district. There was the only one consultant that was not paid. You guessed it. It was the Black consultant. Even after negotiating his contract with the superintendent, the superintendent still refused to pay him. When asked why, she stated that anyone who claims to be giving back to inner-city students should be doing it for free, so why should he get paid? Even though her husband and all her team members were all paid as consultants, and paid on time.
- Where is the corporate board and why are they allowing this behavior to occur? Great question!

The consultant worked for six months without ever receiving income. By the time the charter holder got the message, the school had gone into the winter break, and although she wanted to rectify the situation, it should not have gotten to that point. Eighteenth red flag, minus 20 yards.

Lastly, the most upsetting thing about this district is that they have a state representative at the main campus where the superintendent's office is located. How is it possible that so many adverse decisions can continue to deteriorate the school with state support? Nineteenth red flag, minus 10 yards.

I am not saying the state is involved in any wrongdoings. What I am saying is, if the state is aware of this information, why was it allowed? And if the state was not conscious but was present several times a month, why was it allowed?

I was told that due to low enrollment of fifty students, my students and staff did not warrant state assistance, so therefore, they had to go without for the entire year. There were only 300 three hundred-plus students throughout the school system, so I did not understand the reasoning. The goal should be to end inequalities, not increase them.

I would enjoy remaining in education after the pandemic if possible but never under this type of leadership again, this late into my career. This horrific leadership is why I moved into phase two of my purpose in life—BOLO ICLC. Inner-City Life Coaching.

I developed this non-profit business to continue the fight of; helping inner-city students receive a proper education, graduate with a high school diploma, and ensure they have the proper nourishment needed for learning, at the same time, attempt to provide a smooth transition into adulthood.

Inner-City
Life Coaching

We believe that each individual has the ability to make and shape their lives the way they want. Our coaching strategy allows us to help students establish positive relationships in life and business. When you first start in young adult life, sometimes you need a guide or someone who understands where you are and where you're trying to go. We believe in the power of choice. The choices an individual makes will determine their future. Inner-city life coaching will help you find your solutions to the problems you are facing.

Inner-City Life Coaching offers you the following services:

- We will help you discover what's most important to you.
- We will help you design a plan to achieve your goals.
- We will work with you to eliminate obstacles in your way.
- We will help you conquer your dreams.

Inner-City Life Coaching's three key areas of focus:

- Guidance
- Empowerment
- Improvement

Guidance is the life coach providing the necessary tools and support for you to broaden your viewpoint and open your mind, which will allow you to reach your goals.

Empowerment helps you realize who you are and what your worth is, and you identify your purpose in life.

Improvement enables you to establish a tracking system to evaluate your progress and focus on reaching your goals.

Ronald Alexander found Inner-City Life Coach (ICLC) in March 2020. ICLC's objective is to help high school graduates and adults accomplish their career goals and dreams. If you are considering going to college, but you are unsure of the route you should take, ICLC can help. If you believe in yourself as a nontraditional student or a young adult looking for guidance, ICLC can help.

ICLC is focused on helping individuals who are forced to take a non-traditional route to get their lives back on track. Traditional students who fit the standard model of getting an education usually go to college between 18 and 23. ICLC is fully aware of those individuals who are forced to take an alternative path to success due to life's circumstances. ICLC was established to help younger adults find their way through life.

Challenges and Support

Young adults in Phoenix, Arizona, face some unique challenges when focusing on their futures. Nontraditional students and young adults are more vulnerable to factors that might make them unable to attend school, establish a career, or even start a healthy family. They might be single parents, for example, who must divide their attention between work, family, and school.

Closure

It is truly a pleasure in being able to tell my story about a profession I spent the last thirty years in attempting to make some form of continuous improvement. I will always remain an educator, but I am now looking into taking a new direction in my life.

As I develop this new venture, I will continue whatever assistance I can provide to the educational system whether it be as an administrator, a consultant, a trainer, or a superintendent.

I hope I can also assist in decreasing the number of homelessness our country is experiencing. The homeless population is increasing its numbers due to lack of education, untreated mental illnesses in our youth stemming from drugs, lack of support from our country and families, lack of medical care, and the list goes on.

I want to make sure I spend most of my time giving to those who may be in more need than my family or me. While making sure my own children are as prepared as I can make them for a country that still favors racism, negativity, and hate, I will also provide as much time as allotted to improving inner city family life education and life coaching.

Acknowledgments

I would like to thank God for the ability to put my thoughts on to a paper and hopefully share them with any educator or parents looking for a few answers but cannot find them. My faith has awarded me much success in education, and I will rely on it to lead me as I embark upon new endeavors with this journey of saving our youth.

To my son, who is soon to be king and whom I love with all my heart. I am so proud of him, watching him grow into becoming a well-mannered and respectable young man. His drive and determination will propel him by saving many lives as he enters the world of nursing. I am blessed that as a cum laude graduate from Chandler High School, my son learned the importance of a good education early in life, but I hope he learned even more is the importance of giving back and helping those in need.

To my daughter, who is soon to be a queen and whom I love with all my heart, you continue to amaze me with your creativity and sincerity. While maintaining scholar grades in school and As and Bs since elementary, I look forward to seeing you continue your learning by attending a college that will educate you in your area of career choice.

You are a beautiful young Black lady whom the world has yet to experience, but soon they will see the beauty in you that I have had the pleasure of seeing for sixteen years and counting.

My two brothers, we have shared half a lifetime, and I look forward to spending the rest with you. Thank you for all your support, whether verbal or in silence. I know you are always close by when needed, and I plan to continue calling on you for the rest of my life.

My brother, Charles, has always guided me positively and continues to when needed. I appreciate all that you have done and yet to do.

My brother, William, thank you for all that you have done for me, from raising me as a little brother to buying me my first car. I will always love and respect you for the example you have set for me as a big brother and, in turn, hope that I return the favor. I look forward to seeing you soon.

To my cousin, Cynthia, thank you for showing me at an early age the importance of having a good education. You inspired my drive to attend college at an early age by taking Chill and I to a family day at the college you attended, Hiram University. Seeing you as a teacher helped me in making my final decision on what I wanted to do for a career. Having you in AZ has made things more pleasant for me, as you were the only family I had until I knew Aunt Maggie was out here. Your support and friendship have meant the world to me, big cuz, and I love you for it.

To my brother, Devaughn, thank you for recognizing a talent in me that I have suppressed for so many years that I had almost forgotten that I had. Meeting you was the push I needed to reestablish who I was meant to become. Your support with providing a service to support inner-city students helped me show students that there are people out there who care about their welfare and want to help them as much as they can.

I know your nonprofit will help refugees with seeking the assistance they need with their transition. I look forward to helping with your cause and supporting you with making a difference in the lives of many who are at risk.

Coach Jeffery Rominger, thanks for your support and friendship throughout the academic year 2019–2020. You are a valuable asset, not just to the school but the community and children within. Having someone like you is vital to helping students stay the course and have fun while doing it. You brought light to the students who may otherwise be down. You have always been a dean of the school, you just did not know it.

Claribel Hollywood Rodriguez, my friend. You were the key to much of my success, and I refuse to allow it to go untold. Your assistance and guidance throughout my leadership in the last three years were truly amazing. Your ability to calm me down when I was irrational, lift me when down, make me smile in place of frowning is the reason we experienced much success. I hope that we continue to change the world by working together to provide a service that inner-city students need. Thank you for all your support.

To all educators, administrators, leaders, and parents, thank you for doing your best to educate our youth so that our world can live on for decades to come. The work that you do, although often goes unnoticed unless attached to negativity, will remain as one of the most important occupations needed for the survival of our society.

To my haters out there, I want to thank you for the overtime you have been putting in, hoping the worst for me. I know you could have spent this time with your family or doing more positive things in your life, but in lieu of those, you chose to spend it on me, and for that, I am grateful. You helped me to wake up so I can continue the fight of good against evil. Please keep it coming. I have plans for the next three years. Let me know if I need to inform you of who you are!

Dr. Fuginitti, the Italian stallion, thank you for all your support. Unfortunately, people did not want to see us make a difference with students as we have done before, but please continue doing what's right for our youth.

To the teachers who educated me even when I caused you the headaches you did not deserve, my bad. I am extremely grateful and beneficial for all that you have done for all the other students and me you serviced. I hope that I can return home one day and return the favor by preparing our youth as you have done for me. I cannot remember all the names that I should recall, so I apologize if I miss your name. Mr. Patillo, Mr. Gideon, Mrs. Stewart, Mrs. Bryson, Mrs. Patternini, Mrs. Campbell, Mrs. Talley, Mr. Walker, Mr. Harrison, Mr. Quarrels, Charles Reynolds, Mr. Basha, Mr. Karnack, Mr. Sanda, and all Warrensville staff past and present, thank you.

Vashti Ivy, thank you for all that you taught me about science. I was able to teach for thirteen years about science and loved every minute of it. I hope you are doing well and wish you all the best.

Dr. Suweeyah Salih, my friend, I know you are still doing everything you can to make way for our people, especially our youth. I look forward to working together again and making a difference for our youth by educating them and preparing them for society. I wish you well in all your endeavors and will be reaching out to you soon for collaboration on a positive project for our youth.

To my family. Jaden, you are a born leader who needs the right guidance for reaching success. Your entrepreneur drive will lead you to good things in your near future. Remember to stay humble and keep an eye on your surroundings.

Jacob, you are destined to be whatever you set your mind to. Your intelligence and smooth demeanor will work to your advantage. I am so impressed with your ability to listen before speaking. This is a skill that many adults continue to struggle with. Continue to move forward while planning for the future.

Billy, thank you so much for your trust and for allowing us to grow as a family. My brother and I are so appreciative that we had the chance to connect, and we have always wanted you and your sibling to know how much we love you all.

Jordan, it was truly a pleasure getting to meet you, and I look forward to our next visit. Thank you for meeting with us, and continue to strive for success. I believe you are going to make a difference in whatever you choose to do, and I look forward to seeing your success.

Sarah, I cannot express to you how much I look forward to meeting you. Thank you for always taking the time out to talk to us. Your uncle and I love you very much. You are so beautiful, and soon you will one day be a queen.

Joshua. Hello, nephew. Sorry I could not make it down with Chuck to see you guys, but know that I am so proud of you for serving our country and for beginning your family by starting with marriage. You are the oldest of the cousins, and I believe you are setting a good example for them *all*. Much love, nephew, and I cannot wait to see you.

Remember, family, anyone who fails to plan, plans to fail.

To my brother Luck, golf punisher! Appreciate you bro, soon the student will crush the teacher (hmmm). Wishing you and your Queen, Nichole, the very best.

Ronald Alexander
innercitylifecoaching@gmail.com

About the Author

While working as an aide (tutor) at Westwood Elementary School in Warrensville Heights, Ohio, Ronald Alexander discovered his career of choice, education. His journey began at Tri-C Community College before transferring to Kent State University where he received a bachelor's degree in elementary education in the year 1996.

After receiving his first teaching position teaching science at Kirk Middle School in East Cleveland, Ohio, he continued his education by attending Cleveland State University and receiving a master's in curriculum and instruction in 1998.

The experience he acquired as a science teacher and head wrestling for seven years at Kirk Middle School, has propelled his career for working in the inner city. When you know the importance of community involvement, understanding the challenges students face, seeing and learning the effects of poverty, establishing trust with students and coach, creating a positive culture, and collaboration with other teachers, administration, and stakeholders, you can reach success.

In 2001, he transferred to Bedford Heights and continued his victory in the classroom and as a head wrestling coach in Heskett Middle School.

By 2007, his family and he relocated to Phoenix, Arizona, and he began his administrative career while attending Northern Arizona University and receiving his principal's certification in 2009. Starting as a turnaround coach, he later became a principal then director. Although his expertise is K–8 education, he became a high school principal in 2017 and continued his success by focusing on learning.

Although being a father is his greatest joy, and he always finds time to pray, golf, swim, read and learn, and spend time with his family.

CPSIA information can be obtained
at www.ICGtesting.com
Printed in the USA
BVHW081438290421
606129BV00009B/769